I0847190

COLDHEARTED

Blood Stains and Broken Trust

Lou Garden Price Sr.

URBAN AINT DEAD

P.O Box 960780

Riverdale GA., 30296

No part of this book may be reproduced or transmitted in any form by any means electronic or mechanical, including photocopying, recording, or by any information storage system, without written permission from the publisher.

Copyright © 2023 By Lou Garden Price Sr.

All rights reserved. Published by URBAN AINT DEAD Publications.

Cover Design: Angel Bearfield / Dynasty Cover Me

Edited By: Veronica Rena Miller / Red Diamond Editing by V. Rena, LLC

reddiamondediting5@yahoo.com

URBAN AINT DEAD and coinciding logo(s) are registered properties.

No patent liability is assumed with respect to the use of information contained herein. Although every precaution has been taken in the preparation of this book, the publisher and the author assume no responsibility for errors or omissions. Neither is any liability assumed for damages resulting from the use of the information contained herein. This is a work of fiction. Names,

characters, places, and incidents are either the product of the author's imagination or are used fictitiously. Any resemblance to actual events, locales, or persons living or dead is entirely coincidental.

Contact Author at: paralegal.louprice1@gmail.com (for book editing, and ghostwriting quotes).

Snail mail: LOU GARDEN PRICE SBI 00454309

Delaware DOC 1101

PO Box 96777

Las Vegas Nevada 89193

**See: GettingOut.com/create account

Search Lou Garden Price SBI #00454309

James T Vaughn Correctional Center, Smyrna DELAWARE

For tablet connection. Download the gettingout.com app.

Contact Publisher at www.urbanaintdead.com

Email: urbanaintdead@gmail.com

Print ISBN: 979-8-9886522-5-0

Ebook ISBN: 979-8-9886522-6-7

Soundtracks

Scan the QR Code below to listen to the Soundtracks/Singles of some of your favorite U.A.D titles:

Don't have Spotify or Apple Music?
No Sweat!
Visit your choice streaming platform and search URBAN AINT DEAD.

Currently on lock serving a bid?
JPay, iHeartRadio, WHATEVER!
We got you covered.

Simply log into your facility's kiosk or tablet, go to music and
search URBAN AINT DEAD.

URBAN AINT DEAD

Like & Follow us on social media:

FB - URBAN AINT DEAD

IG: @urbanaintdead

Tik Tok - @urbanaintdead

Submissions

Submission Guidelines

Submit the first three chapters of your completed manuscript to urbanaintdead@gmail.com, subject line: Your book's title. The manuscript must be in a .doc file and sent as an attachment. The document should be in Times New Roman, double-spaced, and in size 12 font. Also, provide your synopsis and full contact information. If sending multiple submissions, they must each be in a separate email. Have a story but no way to submit it electronically? You can still submit to URBAN AINT DEAD. Send in the first three chapters, written or typed, of your completed manuscript to:

URBAN AINT DEAD
P.O Box 960780

Riverdale GA., 30296

DO NOT send original manuscript. Must be a duplicate.
Provide your synopsis and a cover letter containing your full
contact information.
Thanks for considering URBAN AINT DEAD.

Acknowledgments

Thank you God Almighty.

Thanks to all the haters for all the energy y'all give off which I use to motivate myself. The more you dumb nyggaz say negative shit the more copies get sold. So good lookin' out (cornball ass mufuckaz).

Elijah R. Freeman (CEO URBANAINTDEAD.com) youse as real as Huey P., Malcolm X, Larry Davis (Bronx NY - RIP) you know what I'm sayin', homie. M. McClure (COO) thank you, too. I realize how hard you work too. The whole U.A.D. Fam write as hard and as intelligent as you can.

My daughter Xiania you my "heartlovinsoul." My son Lil Lou, you my ribcage that protects my heart LeAndre Christine, my eldest daughter and firstborn you my chest where it all lives at and your daughter (my grandbaby Lay'Anna) is where the cycle, my legacy goes on. I love all of you.

My sister Leana and Brother Chad, Selena, I love and thank you dearly. JaQuan Harris and his wifey 4 lifey Yadi in Delaware I am indebted to you and love you, too.

There's not enough time or force I could put behind

thanking my readers and all of you who have taken time to review and rate my work. I love y'all for that.

Shout to Brook, Piza (Rome), Q, all my dudes at James T. Vaughn Correctional Center. I feel like listing all the dickhead staff but that's a waste of time cuz they exist West, East, Mid-West, Down South – that's like saying to the 12's: "<u>Stop shootin' nyggaz in the street.</u>" But what good thatta do? Fuck these dickhead bastards.

Just lemme leave y'all with this. They took my freedom but not my mind. And a hundred years ago we were bein' persecuted for reading/writing. Killed. Hung. I been where I been for over 22 years now. Wife divorced me. Momz died. A 21 year old son murdered by three cowards up New York. Sea, they want us to weaken and fold and do punk shit in here. Not Shirley Ann Price's son. Find what you are strong at and become the best at it. If you work at it every day, no one can fuck witchu. That's what I have in my heart and mind each day. I am up at 2 AM getting stronger, writing harder. If I can't be there (New York City, etcetera) oh well...

Wherever you're at that's where you make your motherfucking stand. They'll (the state, the DDC, the D.A., haters) despise you even goddamned legacy they never counted on. They wanted me silenced and labeled how they wanted me remembered. Fuck 'em. Fuck 'em all. I get the last word about the person I am.

I love you, dear readers. New Fuckin' label alert:

AUTHOR: Lou Garden Price, Sr.

Paralegal.louprice1@gmail.com

For Xiaa Lou Garden Price, Jr. (1999 – 2021) Don't worry about it, son. I'll mourn you til I join you. Your enemies are now my own. And I pray that Our Lord causes them Great suffering, pain, and destruction. Amen.

Foreword

"Everyone has demons living inside them. Even the angels. Just look at how Satan fell from grace and made an enemy out of God... Probably the worst enemy one could ever make." – Unknown

Part One

Blood Stains and Broken Trust

Chapter One

Newport Gardens Apartments
Brownsville, NY
Monday 3:00 AM

Five-year-old Sage Michael Thomas peeked through the slightly open door where he thought he might locate his mother, father, or maybe even both. He had been asleep on his pissy smelling airbed in the back of the apartment when he was awakened by several roaches crawling on his face, neck, and bare chest. Then, to top it off, a mouse had ran across his legs. They were all licking remnants of the peanut butter and jelly he had eaten the night before.

He was starving all over again and he was in luck because there they both were, on that old nasty brown living room sofa. Daddy was seated with his pants down and Mommy's face was moving up and down in his lap – making wet eating noises. Well, to Sage it sounded like eating noises...

It was only 3:00 AM so it was still dark outside. That meant it was dark inside because Con Edison had turned out the lights. Sage heard Mommy and Daddy arguing about it the day before. In fact, Daddy had whooped her ass really bad. Afterwards, Daddy had given Sage the peanut butter and jelly to eat, no bread.

Sage knew not to bother Mommy while she was "eating" Daddy so he just tried to see better. The only light he had to see with was from two of those tall glass candles depicting pagan sketches of the so called *Virgin Mary* crying. Or *weeping* as the Catholics put it.

The faint candlelight flickered, casting a silhouette image of his mother slurping on his father, Big Kato. Arnesha, his mother, was still a hot piece at eighteen even though she'd had a five year old son at an early age and a dope habit. But that didn't matter because when she walked through the hood, nyggaz was still staring at that chocolate ass she was packing in them jeans. She was bad as fuck.

When Lindsey Lohan, Demi Lovato, and half of them bitches in Hollywood turn dopefiend, pillhead, alcoholic, or whatever, nyggaz still wanted to fuck them hos. The 'hood ain't no different except skin color and economic status. But the pussy remains the same.

"Arnesha! What – who da fuck was dat?" came from the startled voice from the funky sofa he was getting his dick and balls licked on. "I thought you said no one else was here!"

"Don't just stand out there, boy," came the actual voice of his father from the far left. "C'mere!" Sage, confused, walked past the strange man on the sofa who Sage had initially thought was his father, wondering why Mommy was on her knees eating from him. Sage only wore a pissy pamper which his father took off of him, trashed it, and put on a fresh one.

"Can we go to another room?" the strange older Black man asked Arnesha in a whisper. "I'm so close."

"C'mon, baby," she said, starting to get up.

"Nah, bitch," Kato growled from where he sat in the kitchen. "Finish toppin' that greasy ass nygga off right there!" he demanded coldly.

"But the lil nygga," the trick protested, but only for a moment.

"Pay attention to me, honey," she said as she took him back into her warm wet mouth. She was so thick, her chocolate titties were out and he held her head as he hardened fully again. "*Mmm! Glbb! Mmm...*"

"You see ya mama, son?" Kato whispered into Sage's little ear so that neither she nor her trick could hear him narrate what was happening. "She earnin' money for the lights to come on... and so you can have some milk, bread, eggs, and cereal. You want Captain Crunch?"

Sage nodded while keeping an eye on his Mother.

"See, son," Kato continued on. "Truth is, I went to jail and come home to a dopefiend whore. She tells me you prolly ain't even mine. That made me feel so evil I wanted to kill her and you."

Kato, whose real name was Titus White, was no slouch in the streets, but Arnesha was a ho and that reflected on him. Ever since they were both in the 7th Grade together they'd been in love. But when she'd gotten pregnant that changed everything. That pressure, coupled with the fact that neither of them were the brightest students to come out of Wingate High School, Kato had resorted to selling crack. Naturally, that eventually landed him in jail.

During his stay on Rikers Island, Arnesha had began popping Zannies and OxyContin's. Not long after that, she'd started snorting heroin. To support her growing habit she'd sold pussy. Subsequently, Kato was released to see her and Sage living in complete and total squalor at the notorious Noble Drew Ali Plaza Projects on New Lots and Mother Gaston Avenues in Brownsville.

In any event, Kato was a fearless stickup kid by trade so it didn't take long for him to move Arnesha and Sage into Newport Gardens Apartments on Lott and Rockaway Avenues. It was around that time when Kato's probation had been violated and he'd been returned to Rikers Island for a few months.

This time, when he was released, the streets were laughing even harder behind his back because another man had emerged as a possible father for Sage. Now, this ho not only fucked half the whole Brownsville but now Sage was "probably not" his son?

The sticky wet slurping sounds continued.

Glbb! Glbb! Mmm! The loud breathing and her sloppy sucking and moaning sounds had now filled the entire room. The candlelights seemed to burn brighter. *Glbb! Glbb! Mmmm, Mmmm!*

SWWOOOSSSHHH!! A sound similar to a wire hanger slicing through the air at 100 mph. And then, right behind that a flat: TTHHUUMMPP! sound. Something heavy hitting the floor behind the sofa. But Arnesha was currently throating her trick as if her life depended on it. She thought her son had dropped something and ignored it. All that mattered was the dick in her mouth and the $50 he had paid. She was trying to finish him off and get herself a fix.

However, Arnesha felt the moisture of a misty like spray hitting her face and forearm as if it were raining and a window was open nearby. Then, she realized that one second the tricks member was raging hard and then the next he was instantly flaccid. "What the hell, man?!" She complained.

She looked up at his face and she jumped backwards,

screaming as she fell onto her ass, knocking over the littered coffee table! The trick's entire head was missing!

To her left stood Big Kato, a large 6 foot 2 inch, 240 pound young man with curly hair and no facial hair. He wielded a long, sharp, machete in his right hand with blood leaking off the blade. Arnesha trembled and screamed bloody murder when she looked over to her right and saw the trick's head, its eyes open, staring directly at her!

"OH, MY FUCKIN GOD!!!" She yelled and then started screaming.

"Shut yo ho ass up!!" Kato boomed, pointing the machete down at her.

He turned to Sage and for an extended, silent, moment he stared at him. Perhaps he'd contemplated killing him. Kato had lost it. He had the look of a madman in his eyes.

"Every man needs his dignity, Sage," Kato declared to the boy. "Remember dat."

He used his cellphone to pull up Youtube. Once he was filming himself he said, "Aight this must be how the white folks, school shooters, and terrorists do it huhn? Well, everybody, I just beheaded this dirty mufucka... as he was gettin' head by a ho I thought I loved. Take a look..."

He showed the world the decapitated head as best as he could with the darkness in the room. "See? This is my machete, my kill. This is my... I think he's my son. This bitch is his mother – a whore. She fucked all of my boys, I'm a laughingstock. A man needs his fuckin' dignity. So this is how I'm goin' out."

With that, he sat the phone down so it could record his next move. Then, he turned the machete on Arnesha...

When the cops arrived, from the 73rd precinct, he lunged at them with the machete raised in one hand while carrying Sage with the other, as a human shield! He was cut down immediately with a burst of semi-automatic gunfire!

"Hold your fire!!" a yell came.

"Hold your fire!!" someone repeated.

"He has a child!!" a ESU Sergeant bellowed.

Cops discovered that the child had also been shot and that sent everyone into an even greater panic! Sage was rushed to the hospital!

But not even the Youtube video could have prepared them for the shock and horror of what was inside of the apartment.

Chapter Two

Newport Gardens Apartments
Brownsville, New York
Monday 6:00 AM

THERE WAS BLOOD EVERYWHERE.

Absolutely everywhere. The lead homicide detective on the case was Camille Vasquez and as she walked inside of the first floor apartment, and stood in the center of the living room, that's what she was observing.

The body on the sofa, the headless male with his pants around his ankles, still sitting upright. His head on the floor, eyes open, genitals on full display.

The mother, also brutally mutilated, hands missing, feet

severed, plus her head had been chopped off. "Her eyes are closed," Camille muttered.

"What's that, Cammie?" Detective Brad Wannamaker queried as he entered, zipping up a white vinyl protective suit.

Camille stood upright, glancing at the good looking 6 foot tall blond veteran detective. Then, indicating the decapitated heads, "The Black male here, his eyes are open because he never seen the blade comin'. And our female victim here... well, her eyes are closed because she seen it comin'. He chopped off her arms which she used to try to shield herself. *Dios mio.* Imagine seein' your own limbs chopped off and your last thing is squeezing your eyes shut as the machete comes down on your neck like a guillotine."

Camille was only a five year veteran before being assigned to homicide recently. However, it had become clear to the Unit Sergeant, and other detectives inside of the Division, that she had a superior talent for understanding crime scenes and solving murders.

She looked Puerto Rican but she was actually Argentinian. She had shoulder length brown hair, silvery eyes, and very pretty. She was average height, for a woman, and had a provocative figure. She cleared everyone at the crime scene – who shouldn't be there – out.

"Our perp is dead," Cam sighed as she filmed with a small handheld digital camera. "Mom's fellating the BM deceased on the sofa as Dad watches. At some point, the toddler awakes and enters through this door."

Indicating the kitchen table she states, "Dad sits there watching mom perform... judging from the squalor of this place she's a crackhead or dopefiend. We know Titus White is a thug and gang banger. Arnesha here was the boy's mother."

The two homicide detectives stared at each other as Sergeant Matthew French, Lt. Maury Coviello, and Captain Joe Vaughn entered unexpectedly. They slowly looked around and the Captain spoke first.

"This entire fucking this is captured on Youtube!" he boomed with an explosive hand gesture. "And now it's being watched by every schmuck with a cellphone or internet all over the goddamned planet!"

Captain Vaughn removed his hat and handkerchief and wiped the rivulets of sweat from his bald head and face. He was a light skinned Black man with a thin mustache and broad torso. He shook his head as he looked around.

"How does it go unreported that a small boy is living in a dump like this?" Vaughn queried no one in particular as he did a walk through. "Is this a generator?"

Camille Vasquez nodded. "Yes, sir. There's no electricity so our own crime lab had to use generators to light it up."

The Captain inspected the air mattress and room the boy slept in and grimaced at the pungent stench of urine and feces he smelled. "My lord. Does everyone here understand the pressure we're about to face?"

Sergeant French, Lieutenant Coviello, Camille, and her partner listened to Captain Vaughn attentively, nodding their heads yes.

"The beheadings are one thing," Vaughn explained. "First we got a guy out on early probation. They're gonna holler about how he got a low plea deal when Titus White is – or was – a known home invader. Then they're gonna go after the D.A. again for allowing this child to live like this because the probation department *had to* visit before Titus was released, correct?"

"Supposedly," Coviello commented.

"The Department of Socal Services will get ripped for not stepping in," the Captain went on. "And when this knife-wielding maniac charged at officers how did we not see the fucking kid he was carrying as a human shield?!"

"Captain, sir?" Camille spoke up. "Not tryin' to justify... but the guy had a *machete* as he charged. Officers *had to* open fire," she stated sarcastically.

"Well..." the Captain spoke slowly. "After all that kid has lost, let's hope he doesn't lose his life."

"What's his status?" Camille asked.

"He's in surgery," the Captain reported. "Last word I got he lost a lot of blood and... five years old. Shot by the NYPD. Damned shame," Vaughn shook his head solemnly. But it was an act. The same dog and pony show for 99.9999933% of

AmeriKKKan Police. Especially in New York. The NYPD's the most racist and most murderous fucking cops in the world. They're the modern day Gestapo whose methodology has been exported to every city and town in the USA with Black and Latinos in it. Just take a look back... even before Eric Garner...

Anthony Ramon Baez, December 22, 1994 (murdered by a bitch ass Bronx cop); Abner Louima, August 9, 1997, beaten by coward Brooklyn cops, kicked in the nuts, and sodomized-up the anus- with a fucking toilet plunger); he lived but might as well be dead after that shit. Amadou Diallo, February 4, 1999- shot 41 times by 4 Bronx cops.

NYPD hates Black people. If Sage dies, in a situation such as this it's just another nygga dead to those evil mother-fuckers.

Chapter Three

Montefiore Hospital
Bronx, New York
Monday 7 PM

Daphne Garcia stood outside of Sage Michael Thomas's room looking in through the window. He had been out of emergency surgery for only a few hours where doctors labored well into the day to stabilize him. He had started the day out at Brooklyn's Brookline Hospital but once he was out of surgery he was sent to the Children's Trauma Unit at Montefiore Hospital in the Bronx.

Daphne was a Social Worker assigned by The Family Court of Brooklyn to oversee the case file while she stood outside looking in at Sage. When she'd first been told she had to drive all the way up to the Bronx she'd been annoyed. Her supervisor had told her something about the case but there were so many like it, she had become numb.

That attitude may sound cruel and insensitive for a woman in her position to have but there were so many school shootings, children dying by "stray" bullets, cases of severe child abuse, neglect, car accidents, and so much more Daphne sees or watches on the news. Like many people, she's become desensitized from tragedy. It happens so much. Especially in New York City.

"Excuse me," a small blond woman appeared behind Daphne. The lab coat she wore had a nametag on it saying that she was a doctor.

"Yes, hi," Daphne greeted her.

"Doctor Kim Willow, is he your family?"

Daphne shook her head no. "Daphne Garcia, Department of Social Studies, Emergency Division."

Dr. Willow nodded and they both took a moment to observe the small brown skinned toddler laying atop the bed with all the tubes and wires going into and out of him. He wore a small oxygen mask. There was a feeding tube down his nose, taped to his face.

"What's his outlook?" Daphne inquired. "Day to day?"

"I wish," Willow said. "Try more like moment to moment. He's in excruciating pain for a child his size. That alone may kill him."

Daphne gave her the file her supervisor had emailed her. "I've had some of the worst cases you could ever think of involving children... Child abandonment, child abuse, sexual abuse, cases of incest, abduction recovery, and even child abuse deaths where kids have died from injuries, neglect, and malnutrition. But none where a toddler was used as a human shield by a father with a machete. And-"

Daphne choked up. It was too much.

Dr. Willow nodded. "You okay?"

They sat down on a cushioned bench nearby as the ICU nurse entered Sage's room. The petite blond haired doctor handed Daphne some tissue to wipe her tears.

"I don't normally see DSS people cry," Willow told her. "You guys are usually such a hardened bunch."

Daphne Garcia was normally unfazed by all of the pain, death, and tragedy around her life. The 5 feet 4 inch tall, great looking, Dominicana-Boriqua woman of 28 had been born and raised in the Bronx. She had very long hair which was naturally black but was now red. Her sister Maria was a hairstylist. As young girls, they had both aspired to be salon owners, hair & nail stylists, but Daphne ended up obtaining her Bachelor's degree in Sociological Studies and becoming a social services counselor in Brooklyn.

"Where I came from you see so much you choose this work to try to help," Daphne said, tears still in her eyes. "But it's days like this when you realize how helpless you really are. I mean what do you do for a five year old lying there, fighting for his life because his father killed mom, then killed himself, and he was shot by police?"

Dr. Willow lightly patted her on her right knee. "You *pray*. And if you don't pray, then hope."

"If you were to bet your next paycheck on whether he'll make it, would you?" Daphne asked her.

Willow shook her head. "I would not. He's had a great deal of trauma. One bullet shattered his left ankle. He was also hit in the lower abdomen where he suffered intestinal ruptures but no vital organ damage. What worries us the most is that he is so severely underweight. He's five but looks two or three. I mean, god, what were these parents doing?!" she lamented.

Daphne knew it was more of a statement than a question, but she said, "The mother was an eighteen year old drug addict, living in poorly kept low income housing. His father was an abusive animal, in and out of jail, with multiple women under his belt. There are a number of theories of why or what made him snap. We'll learn more in the days and weeks to come," the social worker offered.

Dr. Willow was at a loss for words. Dr. Willow finally said, "Where will he go? I mean... that leg. He'll need therapy. Specialized care. Not to mention his mental healthcare."

"I'll try to locate next of kin," Daphne replied. "No one has come forward yet."

Dr. Willow's jaw dropped. "No one has called social

services after this shit has been broadcasted around the world? No aunts? Uncles? No grandparents?"

"Not on call or email. "Daphne shook her head no to every question. She liked the doctor even more now that she cussed. "However, before I leave I'll meet with the social services here at the hospital and leave my contact information in case someone pops up. But as of yet, we have nothing."

Dr. Willow looked flabbergasted. "Dear God... no offense to you but I have zero faith in the foster care system."

Daphne scoffed. "No offense taken. Me neither. I *abhor* bad parents and loathe bad foster care parents even more because of several reasons. One, I question a lot of their motivations for even becoming foster parents to begin with. It's a for-profit system for another."

"But to take on a kid for a *welfare check?*"

"Girl, please," Daphne waved her off like she was talking nonsense. "It's a *hustle*. Especially now. Obama changed it. There's the welfare check, these parents know how to manipulate daycare benefits, they use these kids to defraud food banks, hopping from one to another so they can sell the food stamps to drug dealers, and store owners and pocket the cash. The more kids the better. They get *Section Eight* Housing and I mean enormous, nice, houses or apartments! As the older kids get older they are used in many cases to raise the younger... I'm telling you it's a game and most play it well. Until they get caught."

"And it's the kids who pay," Dr. Willow said.

Daphne nodded. "I've seen child abuse, sex abuse, sex *trafficking* where the foster mother was pimping out her underaged girls."

Dr. Willow shook her head. "Here? In New York?"

Daphne nodded. "What writer was it that said: *New York; a city inhabited by savages.*"

"Rogers? Dee Brown of *On Wounded Knee?*" Dr. Willow offered.

"Brown," Daphne agreed. Then, sighing, she stood up and handed Willow her card. "My cell number is there, too. Please give me a call if there are any changes in his improvement... or, god forbid if we have to send the poor guy to potters field."

"You mean to Hart Island," Dr. Willow said. "The World's largest mass grave."

With a solemn look, Daphne said, "That's the place."

She went into the room with Willow and bent down to whisper into his ear: "*Mejor, chicito. Get better. Fight. Stay strong. You've come this far. Why stop now?*"

Then, patting him lightly on the leg, feeling his warmth she hesitated.

"Daphne?" Dr. Willow looked at her.

"Yeah?"

The two women looked at each other and it was like they *knew.* Daphne had tears.

"I'll get another chair brought in," Willow said.

"That'll be great," Daphne took the cushioned chair that sat in the corner and pulled it up next to the bed.

Dr. Willow returned with a dark haired male medical assistant following her carrying a large orange cushioned chair. He sat it down on the opposite side of the bed and stood by.

No more words needed to be exchanged. Sage Michael Thomas would not be alone whether he – by some miracle – made it past the severity of his injuries or if he succumbed to them.

Daphne wrapped his small hand around her fingers so he had the energy of human contact. Dr. Willow did the same, bringing a smile to Daphne's face.

Chapter Four

Montefiore Hospital

Friday 12:00 Noon

Daphne's life suddenly went from dull and ordinary to one filled with the cornucopia of emotions that came with the extreme power of love that a mother had for her young. This included that suffocating feeling one became enveloped with at seeing their loved one suffer and try to survive an illness or tragedy that was attempting to claim their life.

As was the case with the rollercoaster ride she was taken on by becoming so involved with Sage and his journey. When his first 24 hours after surgery ended with his survival, all was well and good – so far. The second day passed and Daphne marveled at the small boy's strength. By the time day three was over Daphne was sure he had it in the bag.

However, it was discovered that Sage had an infection inside of his nose and throat possibly caused by the inserting and removal of his feeding tube. He had a high fever first, where baby aspirin was administered. But he went into a seizure which Dr. Kim Willow and other medical staff within the children's ICU section knew how to handle. To Daphne, seeing his little body go through so much took a toll on her faith and she really thought he would not make it out of Montefiore alive.

Daphne was sitting out front of the hospital, trying to get some air when Dr. Willow texted her, *"Where R U?"*

"Out on Gun Hill Road side of the hospital," Daphne texted back.

Dr. Willow appeared and the two ladies sat on a bench alongside the hospital's large walkway.

"I nearly lost it in there seeing him go through that," Daphne told her, holding a hand against her chest.

Dr. Willow took a deep breath. "You are getting really emotionally involved with this child."

Daphne acknowledged her new friend's observation by replying, "He's a *baby*... a *baby*."

The young blond doctor agreed. "Have you been neglecting life at home by being here so much?"

Daphne thought of her fiancé, Armand Daniels. He was a

Black man of 32 who worked at the coroner's office as an assistant to the coroner. He made more money than Daphne and, together, they lived a comfortable life in Brooklyn Heights at a newly renovated co-op apartment building on Hall Street off of Myrtle Avenue.

Since being assigned to the Sage Michael Thomas case she'd spent most of her time at the hospital at Sage's side praying for his full recovery and hoping a next of kin would appear asking for custody. But four days had passed and nothing. She ran her caseload from the hospital breakroom on her laptop and cellphone. Her boss, a Black woman, commended her on the support she was giving to Sage.

"You're talking about Armand," Daphne said. "He understands. He'll be at my hotel tonight in fact."

Willow's eyebrows raised up. "You been staying at a hotel?"

"The city's paying for it," Daphne revealed. "It's a image thing. A lot of political head's surrounding this tragedy. Cops, D.A.'s office, DSS. My role is organic. I've fallen in love with this lil guy. My supervisor loves it."

Dr. Willow looked at her. "I don't question how genuine you are. You're going to try to adopt him."

Daphne smiled. "Is it that obvious?"

"It is," Willow nodded. "It is," Willow nodded. "I suggest counseling for you and your fiance first. You're my girlfriend now and wouldn't want you crashing and burning on this.

That little boy was born in hell and he's still living in it. At five years old I remember a lot... what if he does, too?"

"Okay," Daphne assured her. "Do you have a counseling referral?"

"Of course," De. Willow said. "Let's go back inside. I'll write it up."

"Hey, Doc?"

"Hm?"

Daphne walked slowly next to her. "You givin' me this referral and all... does this mean you think little Sage will live?"

Kim Willow emitted a small smile. "I put him on an antibiotic for the infection. We'll feed him intravenously for now but if we can't feed him down the throat... We'll need another surgery. Let's not even speak it into existence. Despite his challenges, this kid has a big fighting spirit in him. So, I'm cautiously optimistic that he'll live. I won't be surprised if he's out of ICU by Monday."

Daphne had hopeful tears in her eyes. "Okay."

Chapter Five

Hall Street Co-Ops
Brooklyn, NY
Weeks Later

New York City was without a doubt a city inhabited by savages. That went for the era in Indian history that was chronicled by Dan Brown as well as by the most recent great writers of today such as Kwame "Dutch" Teague, Mike Enemigo, Elijah R. Freeman, and Eliza Paige Williams.

Weeks had passed since the unspeakable acts of murder-suicide by Sage's father, Big Kato, which nearly cost Sage, a five year old severely neglected Black boy, his life. But after the extraordinary care of medical doctors at Montefiore Hospital and the powerful love of a beautiful Boriqua-Dominicana social worker, Sage was almost ready to be discharged from care.

Daphne had been awarded temporary custody of Sage by a Brooklyn Family Court Judge. She and fiancé Armand had previously spoke of having children but not until after they'd been married. However, before they could even bring Sage home Daphne was served with an *"Order of Appearance"* in the matter of *Sage Michael Thomas and Daphne Garcia In re to: Custody.*

"Babe, what is it?" Armand asked her as she entered their two-bedroom, two bathroom Co-op apartment.

She gave him the envelope she'd shoved the court summons back into. She ran into the bathroom and vomited into the toilet. Armand found her there on her knees, spitting into the toilet where she'd thrown up her entire lunch. His heart went out to her. He grabbed a cold washcloth and mouthwash which she used to rise and wipe with.

"Who the hell is Irene White-Collins?" Armand asked minutes later, as they sat on the edge of their bed dissecting the custody petition.

"Titus White's mother? Daphne assumed, looking over the petition more closely. "Yeah... she's the grandma."

"I hate to say it, love, but-"

"Then don't fuckin' say it!" She scolded him.

"I wasn't gonna say I told you so or nothin' insensitive,

mami," Armand assured her. "I just think a kid should be with his blood."

She cut her eyes at him. "He *was* with his blood. And I believe family is always the safest bet... but where was she weeks ago before-"

Armand Daniels, a 5'9" man of 165 pounds, brown skinned, looked at his woman with a look of deep compassion on his round face. "Before what? Before we bought all this stuff for him?"

She started to cry and cry hard.

"Damn," he said. "You really love that boy, huhn?" He hugged her and she nodded. He wiped her tears away and begged her not to cry. "I'll tell you what. We'll get a lawyer and fight for him. Who's this old hag to come all late in the game and try to take our Sage away? Fuck that ugly lady."

Daphne cracked a smile through her tears. "You serious? We can get a lawyer to keep him?"

"Mami," Armand said, pausing to kiss her sweet lips. "They realize the cops shot the boy and they probably can get a settlement from the NYPD. Look at the law firm they got."

"I didn't-" she started but stopped as he showed her the law firm and signature on the second page of the petition. "Ohh, they be on TV! All the commercials! What lawyer is going to go against them?"

"All the courts you appear in, *think!*" he urged.

She sat up straight. "Um, we get behind the eightball and call the FOP and let them know we think a plan's in place for this big *Zimmerman Firm* to go after the NYPD for shooting Sage?"

"Babe, for a gritty Bronx chick you sure go soft and shy at the wrong times!" he exclaimed. "Them bastard lawyers probably sought out and cleaned up a drunk drug addict grandma they found in the bar bathroom *sucking* on one for another drink!"

"Damn, baby!" she giggled. "I love when you get all rough!"

"*You* get rough and stop being a pussy," he encouraged her. "Here they come on some low-blow shit, so you go even lower and kick them bitches in the balls. Call the FOP."

"You mean *now?*"

"Now. *Ahora.*"

She called the Fraternal Order of Police in Brooklyn.

Chapter Six

Grandma Crack
Queens, New York

I f anyone thought Big Kato had a screw loose, then meet his mother Irene White-Collins. She was from Jamaica, Queens, and was better known as Grandma Crack by every hustler in the 'hood. Not only was she a crackhead but one very few in the game didn't trust or like. She spent a lot of time between Brooklyn and Queens. Mostly in Queens.

Many of the younger hustlers came to her to learn how to cook up crack. She would also spend hours upon hours packaging an entire kilo worth of crack into dime ($10) packets. She was always paid well.

She didn't do a whole lot of waiting around for these "cocaine lessons" and packing side hustles. That's all they were: side hustles. They kept her high and able to sell crack to keep her bills paid. She lived inside of a well-kept apartment building on 148th Street called *The Labrador Building*. When she'd first moved in under *Section 8* she'd had her own children and then she'd raised their children. Except her youngest son Titus White, who'd lived with his father in Brownsville.

Like everybody else in New York that had TV or the Internet, they had seen the graphic online videos of the murder-suicide horror in Brownsville, Brooklyn. There was no funeral for Titus, just a cremation and small gathering of girls he'd known from the streets and a few gang members. His father and mother had both been there and neither were interested in taking in the injured Sage.

Not until a slick-talking lawyer had come to Grandma Crack's Queens residence dressed in one of the slickest Armani suits she'd ever seen. He had explained how she, Irene, could win a large cash settlement against the NYPD & DSS for not following up on numerous complaints of child abuse/neglect against Arnesha, the city development company that ran Newport Gardens for allowing the neglect to go on for an extended period of time.

There was only one thing that had made Irene hesitate and that was something she'd remembered Titus saying while he'd been locked up the last time. That Arnesha had been whoring for dope and that she didn't think the baby was his.

But this lawyer had come along talking millions of dollars in a settlement. So she had decided to go along with it and take a gamble. But the first thing they would have to do is win custody of Sage.

"You are his paternal grandmother," the older white lawyer had said "The battle we'll have is explaining why you let him stay alone for weeks in the hospital. Why weren't you involved?"

She had shrugged. "Afraid, I guess. I mean, I never even met the boy."

The lawyer had grimaced. "A stranger jumped in. An angel. A Puerto Rican-Dominican woman named Daphne Garcia, a well-respected, well-liked DSS worker. Left his side only to shower at a hotel near the hospital. She's engaged to a Coroner's assistant. Together they have an income of ninety thousand dollars and they have a pair of really good attorneys on loan from the FOP – Fraternal Order of Police."

"What's that mean," she'd asked.

"It means they're also smart," the lawyer Donnie Bruno said. They saw the subpoena, noticed our big name, and figured out that we're going after the big money. The NYPD has deep pockets. They also have big bad wolves for attorneys."

Hall Street Co-Op
Brooklyn, NY
Thursday 12 noon

Chapter Seven

Hall Street Co-Op
Brooklyn, NY
Thursday 12 noon

Donnie Bruno and Irene could do nothing until their court date in 30 days except to prepare. Meanwhile, in the Bronx, after scores of medical staff hugged and kissed his face to say goodbye, Armand and Daphne walked Sage out of the side doors of Montefiore Hospital. They carried balloons, a suitcase, and a few other small items.

Armand secured him in his seat, inside of Armand's gold

Infinity SUV. "He has this scary look on his face," Armand reported to her.

"I'll ride back there with him," she said. "I don't even know if he's ever been in a car safety seat."

She sat next to him and gave him a red Jello cup which he readily took. She found a spoon, opened up the cup for him and fed him the Jello. He was amazed by the cartoon on the TV screen on the headrest and he smiled when she showed him how to put on the wireless headphones. The look on his face was priceless.

"He's so funny!" Daphne told Armand. "He's totally big eyed over the TV and headphones right now."

Armand looked back at them through the rearview mirrors as he drove and felt real good inside. He couldn't remember the last time Daphne had been so happy. She was so overjoyed it was contagious.

Wow, Armand thought. *What a great mother she'd make to my own kids!* Not that he hadn't thought about it before but seeing how she interacted with a child that they were seeking to adopt was tangible proof. It was different than imagining it.

They took him straight home, to his *new* home. Where it was nicely furnished, the lights were on, and where he wouldn't be attacked by mice and roaches as he slept. They walked him into his room first.

"This is all yours, Sage," Daphne told him as she pointed to a race car bed named after Bubba Watson.

"All mine?" he looked up at Daphne and Armand.

He climbed up on it and looked around at his new tricy-cle, football, baseball gloves, Jordan and Air Max sneakers, Timberland boots, a dresser filled with socks, underwear, longjohns, jeans, shirts, a suit, and many, many New York Yankees baseball hats.

"Did you get enough of these, dummy?" Daphne asked Armand putting a blue and gray hat on Sage.

"It's the *Yankees*, they had a sale," Armand shrugged playfully.

She exited to go use her computer and cellphone.

"I'm calling Haymen and McCall," she told Armand as she went down the hall to their own bedroom.

She was referring to Jack Haymen, and Burt McCall, two powerful FOP attorneys with reputations that made other attorneys grimace at the mention of their names. That's how good they were.

"Haymen here," he answered.

"Daphne Garcia."

"Hello there," Haymen said then paused. "I had to pull up an email with a jail record for Irene White and Titus White. Burt McCall, you recall my partner?"

"I do," Daphne answered.

"He's got one of the best investigators ever," Haymen said. "The streets tell her that Mr. White, or Big Kato as he was known, was losin' it because Arnesha had told him that Sage was *not* his son. Arnesha had a number of phone calls with him while he was in jail when this came out and he told several sources on the street this as well."

"So, if he's not Sage's Father..."

"Then Irene's not Sage's grandmother," Haymen finished. "She'd have no legal standing on a custodial matter."

"Hm," Daphne thought it over." Why would her lawyers even waste the time? They *had* to know what youse found out."

"Well, it's a win-win for the lawyers because the case is a big deal," Haymen explained. "There will be cameras at the courthouse. Free publicity."

Daphne's heart was leaping with joy. "Okay, what's your next play?"

Haymen told her what they planned to do. "First we'll get someone to go out to Rikers and listen to all the hours of calls Mr. White made and capture the *'you're not the father'* conversations between him and Arnesha. And more importantly, get a court order to retrieve a sample of Titus's blood from the coroner's office since his body was cremated."

"Awesome," she answered. "My fiancé works in the Brooklyn office of the coroner."

"No, no, no," Haymen said in a protest. "Let's do it by the book. But let me ask you something. We wanna get behind you and stay behind you and what you wish to do with this young man. We're going to need you to assure us that the lawsuits are over with concerning him once we close this White case off."

Armand had come in and heard everything because she was on speakerphone.

"We have no intent-" she started.

"We just want the kid," Armand cut her off. "However, we'll need the city's help with his medical, mental health... education. We'll cap it there."

"Let me make some calls," Haymen stated. "Medical, mental health, and education may need to be spelled out but lemme see how far they're willing to take it."

Once the call was over the two looked at one another.

"You should've pushed maybe?" Daphne said, unsure.

Armand shook his head. "We're city workers, too. We push too hard we'll get zero and be jobless, homeless, and everything else."

Daphne agreed and crossed her fingers. "Man! That was something! The nerve of these people. If Haymen comes in there with DNA disproving she isn't even the grandmother it's *done*! She had no legal standing on a custody claim. And your sexy negotiating skills may get us a kid with a free medical, mental health, and education ride."

"Let's hope," he said, hugging her and grabbing her full dream ass. "I'm thinking you may be interested in taking a ride of another kind?"

She felt his hardness against her and fell to her knees to free him. She was just as hungry for him as he was for her.

Chapter Eight

The Hall Street Co-Ops
Brooklyn, NY

Leading up to their court date having Sage around was an enormous joy. But he still came away walking with a limp and in profound need of physical therapy each day. Because of the temporary custody order, they were able to put him on Daphne's insurance which covered for him a pediatric physical therapist.

It was painful getting that repaired ankle to move again because it had been in a cast since surgery nearly six weeks prior. During physical therapy exercises, Daphne was surprised to discover that Sage didn't cry when his ankle and foot were being bent and twisted by the therapist. A lot of adults came close to tears by during such exercises but Sage only showed discomfort and anger afterwards.

For up to one to two hours after each session, his entire mood would change from being happy watching a movie in the car on the ride over, to anger and silence. When she'd try to cheer him up he wouldn't even look at her. She tried to explain it to Armand.

"I don't know," Armand said one evening after he'd returned from work late. "I'll take him tomorrow and I'll see for myself."

And, lo, and behold, Sage exhibited the same behavior. Armand later theorized that, "I think he's feeling he's being abused or forced to do something he doesn't want to do. And his silence is real anger. He wants to cry but he's been beaten into silence whenever he feels pain."

That was disturbing enough for Daphne to start a search for a child psychologist.

While that search was underway, of less concern to them even, was that Sage would sneak into the kitchen – particularly late at night – and steal food. At first, he would go into the kitchen and eat it there. Daphne, who had taken a leave of absence from her job to see to his medical needs each day, would catch him and correct him each time. She knew he needed structure and love but, again, he'd become angry and cold. He wouldn't speak to her.

She wanted to see exactly what he was stealing and eating. Armand told her not to discourage him from eating because he'd been so underfed. She assumed the boy was going for the salty snacks and sweets. But she had baked a turkey on one occasion. Then, in the middle of the night, she heard him in the kitchen and she went to spy on him on bare feet. He was seated on the floor eating pieces of the turkey he'd pulled off.

On another night she caught him eating her macaroni and cheese; then her meatloaf; he even liked her spaghetti. But he was eating it all *cold!* she thought. So, one night when he was biting into a pork chop Daphne came into the kitchen and said, "Can I have one?"

Startled, he handed her the one he was eating. She put it on a plate and put one more on the plate with it. She put them into the microwave and poured two cups of apple juice. Once the food was heated up she sat one on the table for him and he immediately sat with her to eat it.

"Hopefully these small things don't turn into bigger things," she told her fiancé.

"I'd hate to see what he'd do with a book of matches!" Armand joked.

"That's not funny," she said.

When their court date came they were met at the courthouse by their attorneys. And as they approached the front of the building they noticed throngs of reporters surrounding Irene and her attorneys addressing the media.

"Here they are!" Haymen and McCall were instantly surrounded by reporters.

"Good morning," Haymen smiled charismatically.

"How are you reacting to the Irene White-Collins withdrawal of her of her petition for custody of Sage Michael Thomas?" A *CBS* reporter queried.

"Sage Michael Thomas is doing much better," Mr. Haymen deflected the question.

"She's the grandmother correct?" another reporter tried to bait him.

"Is that an honest question?" Haymen smiled. "*Yes!*"

Inside the courtroom, a Japanese male judge withdrew the petition without Haymen and McCall ever having to submit the DNA evidence that Titus White was not the biological father. They were happy that they did not have to do so because every man who had ever slept with Arnesha could potentially have a claim of paternity which is why Haymen had answered "yes" to that reporter's question. If the question had been answered any other way then that could delay adoption/custody proceedings even further. Which could still leave the NYPD open for a lawsuit.

When they pulled off, Daphne and Armand breathed a sigh of relief. Their order of temporary custody was subsequently amended to full custody. And several months later they filed to adopt Sage as their own.

It would be a move they and everyone that knew them would regret.

Chapter Nine

Five Years Later

Daphne was a woman at her wits end on what to do with Sage. If he wasn't stealing food from other students' lunch boxes at school the police were bringing him home for stealing food from stores. And even worse yet he was constantly fighting with other kids.

She and Armand had gotten married and had a daughter, Lilith. They called her Lilly. She was five years old and the prettiest little girl on earth if they were to tell it. Sage was protective of her on the one hand but he was also too rough with her when they played. Daphne always had to intervene in their horseplay.

On one occasion Sage had been watching an old Bruce Lee movie. He was obsessed with any movies that contained graphic fighting violence. He had positioned Lilith on top of his bed where he'd practiced a well-placed dropkick into the center of her chest. The kick was so hard that it not only knocked her off the bed but smashed the lamp.

At hearing the crashing sound, Daphne and Armand had run into Sage's room and saw Lilly laying on the floor clutching her chest and struggling to breathe. She couldn't inhale so she was panicking.

"What'd you do!!" Armand had boomed at Sage.

Sage had froze up.

Armand had quickly decided to put his mouth over Lilly's, pinch her nose, and blow into it. When it had seemed to get her to breathe on her own they all calmed down. Armand had been so upset that he wanted to have Sage removed from their home.

"Mami, I'm not being mean," Armand told his wife. "But he's too much! The stealing, the fighting, and now look. He's hurt Lilly! She was turning colors!"

Daphne got him to rethink it as they settled in between the sheets for the night.

"As I rethink it I'm going to look for the best place to send him, Armand said. There are great boarding schools that can offer greater structure, balance, and discipline than we can."

"We're gonna just give up on him?" Daphne sadly questioned him.

"No," Armand replied. "He's still our son but he needs tough love. Not coddling which you seem to do a lot of. Where is he gonna go in life with that? In a coupla short years, they'll treat him like a man. I mean cops."

Unbeknownst to the talking couple Sage was listening to the entire conversation. He was not stupid. Not by a long shot. But all he knew was that his daddy was talking to Mommy about getting rid of him.

He walked into the living room, seething with anger and depression. He had voices in his head that he couldn't understand. Crying voices. His own voice he always recognized but it wasn't coming from his mouth. It came from inside his mind. Then there was Arnesha's voice and Titus White's voices. Sage's new mom and dad weren't aware that the ruthless kids at school had shown him the online video of what his real father had done to his mother. Plus, there was dozens of stories on the Internet about him and his real parents. Just because he was Sage Michael Garcia Daniels now didn't matter. Those ruthless fifth graders at his school were computer savvy.

"You're the son of a axe murderer!" they teased him daily.

"Your Mom's a headless whore!" Someone else would say.

Until he blasted somebody in the mouth and then he'd be blamed for the fight. No one saw when they picked on him.

They'd be sorry, he swore. *Mom, Dad, everybody will be sorry.*

Chapter Ten

Garcia-Daniels New House
Mt. Vernon, New York
Christmas

Christmas was a huge deal inside of the Garcia-Daniels household. They moved into an enormous 4-bedroom house in the Mount Vernon section of Westchester. The move happened just two months after the drop kick incident involving Lilly.

Daphne and Armand had big families. She being Latina, used any excuse to come out and party let alone Christmas period her mother and father, sister and nieces, a few aunts, one uncle, and some cousins. She had no brothers. But Armand had several brothers, no sisters, which was perfect for them to mingle! His mother, nieces, nephews, and some uncles and aunts were a welcome sight. The kids immediately had a blast. Gifts were exchanged and everyone seemed to be happy. Many of them had shown up in the night before and stayed all day for Christmas dinner. The men were only interested in the NFL games that were on all day and the NBA game at night between Golden State Warriors and Los Angeles Lakers.

Upstairs, in different rooms, the boys were playing the new XBOX and in the other room the girls had the PlaySta-tion. Daphne's sister Maria was there styling Daphne's hair, taking out the red dye and giving her back her natural brown hair color.

"Is Papo watchin' them boys and girls upstairs?" Daphne asked, concerned. "Sage and Lilly will kill each other if he doesn't."

"Mami, *espera,* you makin' me messy!" Maria snapped on her. "Papo's up there!"

Papo was Maria's man of ten years. They were happy without being married.

"You better be right," Daphne warned her.

Meanwhile, the girls have been inside of the guest room upstairs when Sage wandered in and somehow or another was asked if he had ever played doctor at his school with a girl. Apparently, Daphne's youngest aunt, Elizabeth, had a daughter who was 12 named Liza who had accepted the dare to go into the closet with Sage and play doctor.

Liza had seen the way women sucked on the penises of men on the Internet and she got Sage into the closet. She kissed him and told him how cute she thought he was. She had let other boys at school feel her up before and she liked it.

"Are you scared?" She breathed hotly as she removed his clothes. "How old are you?"

"Ten," He said, sporting a bone.

She looked at his manhood. "Only ten?"

"And three quarters," he added.

"It's big for somebody that's ten," she whispered, encouraging him to lay down.

She poked her head out of the closet and threatened her cousins and everyone else. "We're not in here. Nobody better say nothin'!"

Next thing...Sage was experiencing something that he knew he shouldn't be. And he just didn't want to end up in any trouble. But even though they were cousins by adoption Liza had him playing more than the kissing game. They was playing "Doctor" now.

First they were kissing. Then Liza who was in control must really love him because that's how they grown-ups found them. Sage was confused. *How are we in trouble for kissin' and huggin' and humpin' around? Sure did feel good!*

Chapter Eleven

This Christmas Inferno

Mt. Vernon, NY

"Sage you need to talk to me," Armand was saying to his son. "They can have you locked up for this."

Classic Sage, he shut all the way down after being yanked off of Liza by Daphne and Maria as if she were the victim. And once Elizabeth heard about it, she actually shouted in Spanish about *"castrating that black spook"* which made Daphne go off. The term was racist and uncalled for.

"Did you just call him a *spook*?! She shouted angrily. Them girls up there said they were playing doctor in the kissing game so I doubt if it was any *rape*! Liza ain't no angel!"

There was complete pandemonium in the home so Armand sent everyone packing, except for Elizabeth and Liza. He wanted to try to extract the truth.

"Son, I'm on your side," Armand told him in an evenly toned voice. "Please, man, talk to me?"

In another room Liza was pushing out fake tears and claiming that Sage had forced her to try sex. Elizabeth wanted to involve the police but Daphne begged her to at least wait.

"This is nuts," Armand said to Daphne's mother's younger sister. "It's late, Aunt Elizabeth. It's Christmas. We all been drinking. And they are both kids under our supervision. Go home for now, get some sleep, and we will all wake up to fresh minds tomorrow."

Daphne agreed with that. "I've seen these kinds of cases. Even if he's arrested he'll be released back to us within a couple of hours. And Liza will have to do a super-intrusive rape exam and interview. So, everyone should sleep first."

Elizabeth conceded and gathered up her and Liza's belongings. She and Lisa left the residence close to midnight.

Armand was above upset. "Mami, this does it for me. You did say you heard that little girl saying 'stop' right?"

"Well he's a little boy," Daphne countered.

"He's big for his age," Armand pointed out. "Liza is much smaller."

"I..." Daphne put her head down. "I heard *stop* but I didn't hear *no*."

Armand just shook his head. "Let the cops figure it out. I don't know what else to do with him. What if Lilly's next?"

Daphne was so upset that she cried herself to sleep.

Sometime, in the wee hours of the morning, the Christmas tree burst into flames and the fire quickly spread from the curtains to the ceiling and upstairs.

There were screams.

Hellish, nightmarish screams. The kinds usually only heard in movies. By the time the fire crews arrived on scene there wasn't anything anybody could do the house was literally a towering inferno.

The fire crew believed at first that everyone inside of the house had perished. But a lone fireman discovered two children pounding on the inside of the garage door covered in ash and soot.

"Good God!" The Lieutenant shouted when he saw them. "Get 'em in the ambo outta the goddamn cold!"

Later the bodies of Armand and Daphne were found in the upstairs hallway. They had died of smoke inhalation before the fire could even get close.

"What's your name, son?" the blond EMT asked Sage.

"His name is Sage Michael Garcia-Daniels," Lily answered for him. "He's my big brother."

"He can't speak?" The EMT asked.

Lilly looked at Sage. "Not when he's upset."

The EMT nodded. "Okay."

"He save my life," Lilly said.

"Aww," the EMT nearly began crying at hearing her little voice.

The children were transported to Mt. Vernon Hospital for treatment of smoke inhalation and mild shock.

Chapter Twelve

Mt. Vernon Hospital

When Maria Garcia, Daphne's 24 year old sister heard what had happened her heart immediately turned dark against Sage. She vividly remembered the rape accusations made against him, and she suspected him of starting the fire.

"Let me get this straight," Sergeant Jeffrey Govan of the Mt. Vernon Police Department said. "That ten year old boy, the adopted son of Mr. and Mrs. Garcia-Daniels, *intentionally* set that fire to cover up raping twelve year old Liza Garcia? Is that what you're telling me?"

"I think so," Maria stated as they stood outside of Sage and Lilly's hospital room two days later.

"I'm sorry, ma'am," the sergeant said. "But five investigators think a space heater was too close to the Christmas tree and do not suspect arson. And a ten year old boy raping a twelve year old girl? That's a headline!"

Maria was not convinced about the space heater. It was too convenient. Plus, she had heard many dark sides surrounding Sage.

The Department of Social Services arrived regarding the Garcia-Daniels children. Maria was adamant about not wanting Sage. No way, no how, never, she said.

"Do you have other family who will take him?" the raven-haired Jewish Woman asked as Maria sat across from her inside of the Mt. Vernon Hospital Social Services Office. "I mean he is the adopted son of your sister, Daphne Garcia."

"Well, Armand has family," Maria pointed out, continuing to refuse to take Sage in. "Miss Thornberg that child is a *demon seed*. I cannot and will not- -"

A firm knock came on the glass portion of the door.

"Come in," Grace Thornberg looked up and waved in her secretary.

"I'm sorry but a lawyer is here for Mr. and Mrs. Garcia-Daniels?" she said it like a question of what to do with the lawyer.

"Send him in," Grace told her. "This may be interesting. Care to stay?"

Maria shrugged. "Maybe the lawyer can take the demon." Grace scoffed.

A man with curly black hair, dressed in a dark gray suit, red tie, and a long black overcoat was ushered into Grace's office. "I'm Tom Harvey with *Mills, Harvey & Gibson Law Firm*," he introduced himself with a handshake.

"Grace, DSS," she said. "And this is the sister of Daphne Garcia -"

"Oh, Maria Garcia?" Tom asked, sitting down.

Maria nodded. "Do I know you?"

"No, but I'm pressed for time," he smiled and opened a briefcase. "Your sister, may she rest in peace, has a number of life insurance policies on the lives of herself and her husband that will be coming through my office once cleared through each agency. Those policies are in the names of... Lilith Ana Garcia-Daniels and Sage Michael Garcia-Daniels in the amounts of... Well this one is $50,000 per each child."

Grace looked at Maria, who was all ears.

"*Policies,* you said?" Mariastated.

Tom nodded. "Six hundred and fifty thousand dollars in life insurance will be paid out, into a trust, for each kid, set up by your sister naming you a possible trustee. In her Last Will and Testament, she made you Guardian of her children if anything were to ever happen to her and Armand."

"Armand signed off on this?" Maria asked.

"He was with her, yes," Tom answered, handing her some paperwork to sign.

"One point three million in insurance," Maria muttered as she scanned the files. "*Only* if I'm the custodial guardian?"

"Well," Tom shrugged. "Armand named his oldest brother as second in line if you wish to pass."

Maria knew that she could do wonders with whatever "extras" the trust could provide. She thought about passing up on taking in Sage and she wrestled with it. The kid was bad inside and out. *Poisoned* from the great-great-grandparents on down. She'd heard nothing good come from his bloodline and now his name was *Garcia*.

"Ma'am?" Tom looked at his watch.

"Oh, yes, yes." She signed all of the paperwork and agreed to come to his office to finalize things once all of the insurance money was paid out.

"We'll handle everything," Tom said as he rose from his seat. "And the bank will email you further details of the trust."

Grace Thronberg sat back in her chair after he exited. "So, Sage is going home with you now I take it? Or should I find someone else to take the money?"

Maria put her copy of the papers she signed away and stormed out of Grace's office.

Grace shook her head. "That woman has no shame."

Chapter Thirteen

The New House
Mt. Vernon, NY

Maria had a hard time focusing on Sage, Lilly, her salon or her own life as she helped the family bury her sister. At the funeral service Sage never shed a tear but Lilly was inconsolable. Sage was noticeably close and protective of her and it softened Maria's heart some to see that because Lilly was an extraordinarily beautiful little thing and she leaned on Sage. She would need him terribly.

After the funerals, Maria learned that there was a separate insurance policy that covered the house fire so she started there. She decided to rebuild the house and move to Mt. Vernon because it beat the hole-in-the-wall apartment she stayed in above her hair salon in the Bronx. Sage and Lilly moved in with her until their new house was built.

Six months later the move occurred and the house had been totally transformed. It was now a 5-bedroom, 4-bathroom, 6,500 square foot Mediterranean-style flat that stood out from all the rest. All of the insurance money had been paid out for the children so Maria did not hesitate to use some of it to build a fortress for herself and her sister's kids.

Not long after they had moved in they were visited by Elizabeth and Liza. Elizabeth was Maria and Daphne's mother Lupé's youngest sister. Liza was the innocent-but-not-so-innocent 12 year old Catholic schoolgirl who had cried rape against Sage over the Christmas holiday, now aged 13.

Maria's man of ten years let them in as Maria was preparing dinner for the family. Sage and Lilly - both 11 and 6 years old now – were in their rooms or somewhere in the enormous new residence.

"Papo que paso, flacco?" Maria frowned at him. (*What's up, man ??*)

"*Escucha, Princessa,*" Papo told her as he led them to the living room. (*Listen to them, baby*).

Papo was a construction worker and Maria guessed Elizabeth seen him and begged him to take her to Maria because

Maria hadn't been answering her calls. Maria had heard that many people in her family were blackballing her because she had taken in the "monster" that had raped Liza. Not only that but then word got out - from Armand's family Maria presumed - about the life insurance money Armand and Maria had thoughtfully deposited into a trust account for the kids worth more than a million dollars. Now Maria's family was looking at her as if she'd done something sideways and doing a lot of dart throwing behind her back.

"Liz," Maria said as she dried her hands with a paper towel. They all sat down in the living room.

"Maria," Elizabeth, a chubby good looking woman of 36, long black hair, and dark brown eyes spoke to her niece with a humble, contrite, attitude. "It seems we have something we need to say."

Maria and Papo sat next to each other on the black leather sofa. Elizabeth sat next to her daughter on the matching sofa across from them. Maria's eyes shot to Liza when her mother said "we" twice in the same sentence.

"I'm listening," Maria said.

"*Flacca,*" Elizabeth nudged Liza with an elbow.

"Yo mentiras," (I lied) she said in a small voice.

Maria saw Sage enter the living room and Liza Floze.

"About what?" Maria asked her.

"Him," Liza pouted.

"Him who, what, I'm not doin' this with you, Liza," Maria

raised her voice at the now 13 year old Liza. "Spit it all out while he's here, we're here ..."

"I lied about the rape," she admitted. "I was... we was messin' around and started... I was sayin' stop cuz it was hurting but... he didn't want to do it. I wanted to see what sex was like." She was embarrassed, her eyes were down.

"And?" Elizabeth demanded.

Liza looked between Sage and Maria and said, "I'm so sorry."

Maria visibly inhaled deeply and exhaled slowly. "That was some mean, conniving, shit you did, Liza. You know what you could've cost him? Matter fact Daphne died thinkin' he did that! And so did Armand."

Maria couldn't even stand to look at her cousin anymore. The tears welled up in her eyes as she got up to hug Sage. As she did, Sage stared at Liza without anyone seeing him because Maria was all but smothering the boy inside of her bosom. She'd thought he was a rapist.

Elizabeth and Liza stood up and walked towards the front door.

Maria wiped her tears and said, *"Tia,"* (Auntie). "We're having tacos and rice. Let's break bread, pray, eat - not in that order?"

Elizabeth was uneasy. "Yeah - these two." Indicating Sage and Liza. "I don't want them.... you know."

"They're kids." Maria reasoned. "And we all explored."

Papo, who'd been quiet agreed. "Y'know as boys all of my brothers we'd all stand on the curb and see who could spit loogies the farthest. One time this lady cop was ridin' by on a bike and got her! Man, we had to run our asses off to get away because if our

Dad found out - shit, man, I'd be dead!"

Everyone laughed at that.

Hearing the commotion Lilly came out of her room with the Calico Kitten they had bought not that long ago. *"Prima!"* Lilly exclaimed at seeing Liza.

"Primita!" Liza smiled and the two girls embraced. The kitten jumped down and ran off to the kitchen.

Later, after dinner, as Maria and Elizabeth spoke about bringing the family back together Liza saw Sage in his room sitting on his overstuffed chair about to play video games.

"Sage," she said in a quick whisper.

He looked at her. She was so pretty.

"You think about me?" she asked.

He nodded.

"I always think about it." she said. "Everyday I think about it. Even at Confession."

"Confession?"

"Nevermind." She peeked out of the room to the hallway. "Tell Lilly to get Maria to bring me. Meanwhile here's my cellphone number."

Then she kissed him, sticking her tongue all into his

mouth while her hand reached straight down into his sweat-pants and stroked his hardening penis until it throbbed so much it hurt.

"Call me cousin Sage."

Then she hightailed it out of there before they got caught.

Chapter Fourteen

The Following Year
Mt. Vernon, New York

Sage sat inside of his room watching the old video, long since banned from Youtube.com of Big Kato's tirade and subsequent killing of his mother. As he rode the city bus to school he watched the video over and over on his cellphone. Like many kids his age he was computer savvy and therefore knew how to create and hide email and online content with no problem. He had started out slow but once he'd gotten a taste of reading and writing that's all he liked to do.

Since he got into a lot of fights he became good at it but he fought bigger and older kids so he lost most of his battles. Each time Papo and Maria got wind of him fighting, or anything he did for that matter, they would discipline him by making him do extra work around the house or ban him to his room without his electronics. However, he would pick up the Encyclopedia Brittanica or Animal Atlas and read.

Papo had weights and gym equipment in the garage and showed Sage how to make use of everything in there. Sage was steadily bulking up. He wasn't that 5 year old runt he used to be. He was making a name for himself everywhere he went whether Mt. Vernon or around his Garcia family members in the Bronx or his Daniels family members in Brooklyn.

"C'mon, boy!" Liza jumped up and slapped the side of the bus window where he was sitting.

"Damn!" he cussed and jumped up, nearly missing his stop.

He got off the bus by ringing the bell and the driver opened up the rear double doors. Liza grabbed his hand and pulled him away from the high traffic area near Mt. Vernon Middle School where he could be recognized.

"You came!" Sage blurted.

Sage, now 12, was supposed to be going to school on the yellow bus but he and Liza had been trying hard to get together alone for nearly a year. They had been calling, texting and emailing forever it seemed. Even when she'd visit him and Lilly, Maria was always too close for anything ever to happen. But Liza had finally gotten up the nerve to skip school and come to him.

"I couldn't help it," she said as they stopped in front of an apartment building. She put her slender arms around his shoulders, and they kissed.

"Mmm." She tasted like her strawberry lip gloss. Sage couldn't believe a girl so pretty wanted him so much.

"What?" she giggled.

"You're so pretty and taste so sweet."

She blushed. "My heart's beating so fast!"

She wore her Catholic school uniform consisting of a gray pleated skirt that came six inches above the knees, high white stockings, a white shirt and blue sweater. She

looked at the apartment's front door and an older man came out. Before the door could close, she caught it and they want inside.

"Who you know here?" Sage asked her.

"Nobody but we can't stand outside cuz the cops will see us and ask why we ain't in school," she educated him.

They got onto an elevator and rode it all the way up to the 18th floor. From there they found the staircase and walked up to the "Emergency Exit" where they sat down at the top.

"Take your jacket off," she said quietly.

He removed his jacket and she laid it out like a blanket. She did the same thing with her sweater and used his bookbag as a pillow. Once their makeshift bed was made she turned shyly to him and kissed him. He kissed her back hungrily, no longer that ten year old boy in the closet but twelve now and alot stronger.

"You got bigger and everything, Papi," she breathed hotly as she licked his lips and bit them.

They just decided to make out with each other for a while and be close. Liza had a whole lot to talk about such as the fact that she had no father around. She had always known who he was but he never cared. Carlos Juan Jaramillo-Garcia had dealt with Elizabeth when she was very young and living in the Dominican Republic.

The two lovebirds made out some more and poured their hearts out. Then Sage wanted to make it clear. "You my girl and just my girl?" Sage asked.

She climbed on top of him and stared into his dark eyes. "Yeah, right, all them girl friends in Mt. Vernon you got?"

"No girlfriends." He shook his head no. "No sex."

"Huhn? No sex?" She asked as if he was some kind of weirdo. "My whole school has sex."

They got dressed and sat next to each other.

"You wanna be my man?" She asked him. "I mean really my man and everything?"

"You my cousin already," he said shrugging. "I love you – and you *know* I love you. And you a real pretty girl who loves me. I'll kill a nygga for my girl."

"Mmm," she kissed him and ran her hand through his wavy hair. "Whattayu know about killin'?"

He pulled his phone out and played for her the video of

Big Kato beheading his mother. The video even showed Big Kato running out the front door to lunge at officers with the machete raised in one hand while clutching Sage with the other.

"I walk with a slight limp because I was shot in the leg," he pointed to the old wound. Then he pointed to his abdomen. "And here. I was shot by the NYPD at five years old."

"I kept hearing about this!" she gasped, her small hand over her mouth as she watched the video from his phone.

He showed her many news accounts of the infamous murder-suicide: *CBS News, CNN, ABC World News, NBC News, Fox News* and many other outlets. *New York Times, The New York Daily News, The New York Post, Don Diva Magazine, Straight Stuntin' Magazine, Kite Magazine, Thick Magazine,* and more.

She stared at him. "Youse a gangsta nygga. You got bullet holes. Ya Dad was-"

"That mufucka whatn't my Dad," he harshly corrected her. "My Dad would've *protected* me."

She nodded. "Like you'll protect me?"

He pulled her close to him. "Are you my girl?"

She nodded again. "Yes. Yes I'm your girl, Sage."

They exited the building and headed to the bus stop on Post Road.

She looked a little worried. "The bus is going to take too long!" She whined.

He reached into his pocket and gave her what cash he had. "I have cab money."

"That saved my life!" she gushed and hugged him tightly.

She was able to catch a cab that was about to leave his school. He went on in to get a late pass. For the remainder of that day all he could do was think of the prettiest girl he had ever laid eyes on.

Too bad she was his cousin.

But now she was his girlfriend, too.

Chapter Fifteen

Liza and Sage
Mt. Vernon, NY

Mt. Vernon sat right on the northern border of the Bronx. Maria sent Lilith to a Private Montessori school for girls not far from where they resided in Mt. Vernon. Papo had talked her out of sending Sage to Private school because he got into too much trouble at public school.

"You'll be better off shampooing a pig and putting a clean white dress on it," Papo said. "Don't waste the money. Let him make his bed."

"It's his trust," she reminded him.

"Well," He paused to think. "Send him to psychotherapy again."

"It's useless," she sighed. "He shuts down. He won't let no one in. And he won't take any more medication."

There was a group of Bloods that controlled the area of South Mt. Vernon and north Bronx which is where Sage and Liza started to frequent together more often. It made better sense. Elizabeth and Maria grew more and more comfortable with Liza taking the subway to the Westchester Bee-Line bus which came straight through Maria's neighborhood. Lilly loved Liza and Maria welcomed the teenage beauty over anytime now. She would even babysit Lilly whenever she was asked because she looked to be so outside of Sage's league now that she was in high school. She was a real looker. And Sage was more interested in hanging with his newfound Mt. Vernon friends than anything. He definitely wasn't going to be stuck babysitting his little sister when the whole move was designed to get Maria to call Liza over.

"Me and my boys wanna go to the movies in the Bronx," Sage dropped on Maria and Papo as they were getting dressed to go out dancing.

"And get back at two in the morning?" Papo scoffed. "Hell no. Mt. Vernon has movie theatres. You may be big for a kid but you're still a kid okay, Papi?"

"What time to be home?" Sage asked.

"Ten thirty," Maria said kissing his cheek.

They would drop him off at his friend Chubby's house, wave at Chubby's mother-

Tanya Taylor - and drive off. Chubby and several other boys in their clique would meet up at the movies and Sage would leave in a taxi making it home to Liza.

"Lilly asleep?" Sage whispered as he entered.

Liza flew into his arms, passionately kissing him and embracing him. "That girl is knocked out. Come on."

From that point forward they could not control how they felt for each other. The thought of a condom never even came up. They each got to enjoy the beauty of one another unsupervised. He was so in love with the pretty Puerto-Rican-Dominicana that he wished that he could count every hair on her head. She had hair that grown women worldwide were robbing the shit out of horses for! (Leavin' 'em freezing like a motherfucker out back). Liza had that long illustrious jet black wavy hair that fell to the center of her back. Lilly, her cousin had the same exact long, thick hair. The crazy thing about it was that Lilly's father was Armand, a Black man. Lilly was as tan-white as Liza which is why Daphne and Armand named her Lilith, "Lilly" for short. She was as "white as a lily" when she was born.

Liza and Sage were sex crazy for each other there was much more to them. It wasn't just "young love" at play between them but there was a 75 year old's maturity in understanding hearing, listening and being real friends. Not everyone can attain those qualities and blessings in their relationships.

Liza loved to be held and even more than that she loved to be kissed. Fortunately Sage had no qualms about kissing her.

"You should call and tell them you're home," she suggested as the clock was about to strike 10:00 PM.

He found his cellphone as she gathered her clothes and went to shower and blowdry her hair. When she returned she was fully dressed. Sage was nowhere to be seen. She checked on Lilly first. She was sound asleep.

She went to the living room and Sage was standing in the foyer with Chubby who was more Liza's age. Chubby wasn't chubby at all. Liza would later hear that he had been a chubby baby and the moniker stuck. Chubby was 5 feet 6 inches and wore braids. Standing next to each other the two boys looked the same size. What she saw made her curious but she didn't say anything.

Sage put several items inside of a black bookbag Chubby had. One of those items looked like a gun.

"Dang, who she?" Chubby asked when he saw Liza.

"*Ay!*" Sage snapped Chubby back to attention. "You worry 'bout what you have to worry 'bout!"

"Aight my nygga. One." Chubby left right after that.

Sage turned to her.

"You call Papo and Maria?"

He nodded. "They'll be here late."

She thought about that gun all night.

What was Sage into? Whatever it was it made her nervous . . . and turned her on at the same time.

Chapter Sixteen

Blood Bugout / Taizhan
Croton On The Hudson, NY

Bugout's blood was boiling. He was responsible for repaying nearly \$170,000 to P-Man and the Almighty Black P. Stones in Brooklyn. P-Man was a West Coast Blood with roots in Chicago. His entire reputation was built on how he tortured and murdered and kidnapped nyggaz who crossed him or his crew.

Bugout and his squadron of Bronx P. Stones had taken over the cocaine, heroin, and K2 trade in the north Bronx, and entire south Mt. Vemon territories. They had chased out all the major competition: the Crips, "other" Bloods and they even managed to shut down the MS-13 in those areas.

Some of the smallfry dealers still got away with selling on the territory but they risked having their homes invaded and even put their families at risk of being kidnapped, beaten or harmed in some other manner.

Word came to Bugout from his main girl Taizhan - a Jamaican-Chinese beauty with gray eyes, light skin and a talent for numbers - that the count had been off for all the drug sales for weeks now.

They lived in a $3000 per month highrise apartment in Hollow Park, Croton On The Hudson, overlooking the Hudson River. Bugout was a 5 feet 11 inch tall killer with Blood gang tattoos all over his body and face. He'd come a long way since being released from state prison five years before. He had taken the rap for the brother of P-Man over some drugs and a gun found in his car. The Feds had tried to get Bugout to give in on the lie that the contraband was his but he'd stood firm.

Once he'd been released from prison, at age 25, P-Man had rewarded him with a monstrous California connect which consigned Bugout all he needed to supply his

gang and territory. He'd had to kill to carve out that territory and now someone was fucking up his count? P-Man had been clear about the consignment work:

I appreciate what you did for my brother, Blood, P-Man had warned him. *But I don't do charity work. You gettin' rewarded with my cartel connects. El Chapo coke, Afghan dope, and one free arsenal of weapons. All drugs are consignment. Only take what you can handle. I'm only tellin' you once ... never, ever, fuck me over. Understand?*

Bugout had agreed and ever since then he'd kept a stash of $500,000 put up. And right now, he was into P-Man and the Brooklyn chapter of the Almighty Black P. Stones for $170,000. With all of his other debts combined in his other business ventures he was drowning. And, if he wasn't able to pay P-Man he could lose a body part or even worse.

"Whattayu mean sales been off for weeks now?" he asked the statuesque exotic nymph as she lay on her stomach wearing light gray cotton boyshorts that said "DADDY" on the back. She wore a white tank top as she typed on the laptop. She crossed her feet at the ankles but he could still see her mesmerizing pussy print from where he stood applying baby oil on his nude body following a shower.

"I keep averages on all the ocran sales," she said, saying the word "narco" backwards. "Over the past ten weeks we've dropped two percent, four percent, then only a week later we dropped *eight* percent... And ten weeks since the two percent dip we've lost *eighteen* percent. If you round it off to twenty percent against that $170k that's $34k lost."

As he listened to the 23 year old, 5 foot 10 inch tall, bombshell he couldn't help but feel his manhood stand straight up at attention. Her pussy print showed a darkened damp spot where she was leaking at. And the way her boyshorts rode so high up in her bootycrack was insane. She had tattoos of hearts and roses going around one leg up to her asscheek and Poison ivy twirling all the way up the other until it wrapped around her body. It was decorated with red flowers all over to signify her own involvement with her man in the Blood gang.

"So…" he said slowly. "I smell a fuckin' rat."

She turned to him and noticed his long, thick, veiny penis. "Yeah. Me, too. But, no word comin' in from the streets."

"Put word out," he said, anger lacing his words. "I want whoever taken money like this off our plate made an example of."

She sent out an encrypted text to Blood Nimrod and Blood Bain the capo and lieutenant of Bugout. They would immediately carry out his orders and have answers soon enough.

"You wanna take care of this, Blood Baby?" he pointed at his hardened piece of wood.

She closed the laptop. "My pleasure, Blood Daddy."

Chapter Seventeen

Rock
Savage Hoods HQ
Mt. Vernon, NY

Chubb's older brother Rock was the leader of a gang known as *Savage Hoodz*. They started out as a rap group but several of its founding members had even been killed or are doing big numbers in the pen. Rock had gotten lucky. The 6 foot 4 inch, 18 year old dark skinned man had been shot at The Red Circle, a popping nightclub/skating rink up in the northern Bronx.

The Red Circle had been sued by Rock's family. To avoid litigation the club owner quickly agreed to cover Rock's medical bills and pay him $10,000 per month for a year. Rock finished high school and laid low with Chubb, Dojo, Shadow Warrior, Choir Boy, Wolfman, Orca, Tommy Gunz, HK, Mac-11, and a group of Savage Hood Girlz.

Rock could have easily put guns in all of these wild ass young nyggaz hands but inside of their circle of gangstas were something even more effective than guns: criminal masterminds. These kids had the gift of computer technology, hacking and encryption cracking under their belts. Not all of them but enough of them. Once Rock had gotten his hands on that lawsuit money he had invested it in his own loft apartment and loaded it with the very best he could buy in computers, hardrives, all the software he would need and much more. The loft was enormous.

Chubb and Sage were the only ones allowed to help at first but they worked hard to put it all together. The loft was on Cedar Street and Briar Drive, a clandestine industrial section of Mt. Vernon right on the border of the Bronx. As *Savage Hoodz* HQ came together Rock had leased a second loft in the same area. That one was more for everyone to hang out at, sleep at, and party at.

Rock had called a meeting at HQ to discuss an incident involving Orca getting jumped by a group of Bloods at *The Palladium* this past weekend. It happened on the night that Liza had observed Sage place a gun into a backpack Chubb had left with.

"W'sup, Sage?" Rock asked him as they did the Savage Hoodz style handshake-hug.

Sage had arrived in a brand-new Honda Elite which Maria had bought for him. It was all blue and he dressed in all blue with the NY Yankee fitted hat and Alex Rodriguez jersey to match.

"You all blue like you crippin' now, nygga," Chubb said as he handshake-hugged Sage.

Sage turned around and in one pocket he flew the all-black Savage Hoodz Flag, which secretly stood for "Pirates" or, in their case, online pirates. In his other back pocket he flew a bandana that looked like the $100 bill.

"W'sup, cuz?" Sage threw up them C's. He also did his perfect rendition of the Cripwalk. "I fuck wit them Crips before I fuck wit them Bloods. You know I bleed blue but I ain't a Crip though. Savage Hoodz all day here. Where Orca at?"

Everyone was there already. Sage pushed his motor bike over to a corner and joined the others. He didn't expect the girls to be there but they were. Sonja, Alejandra, Shay, Joyce, Blue Eyes, Diamond Girl, Bhad Barbie, Sunny, Ava Applez, and her girlfriend Juicy P.

There were enormous sectional sofas and huge over-stuffed chairs decorating the spacious living room area so there was plenty of room to sit for everyone.

"We started this clan of ours as a rap group but shit evolved into something else," Rock started after he turned off the giant 86-inch curved HDTV. "Most of y'all is still in middle and high school. We all know how to sell coke, dope and pills, etcetera. But we know it's a lot safer to do all that shit and more from a laptop. We can pick and choose: dope, coke, pills, guns, credit cards, even banks, if we want. We can rob any bank we want wit no gun."

Rock lit up a blunt and passed it with an ashtray to his left. And lit another and passed it to his right with another ashtray. Then he packed a bong bowl and hit it before passing it.

"Orca," Rock pointed at the big dark skinned 17 year old with the pink birthmark on the left side of his face. Since it was so big and covered his entire left side someone had teased him one day in grade school and called him *"Orca."* When his mom had heard of this she'd encouraged him to embrace that name for it was a great and, honorable name. When he'd asked why she'd said *Because the Orca is the wolf of the sea, an apex predator also known as the Killer Whale.* Emboldened by that information he'd demanded everyone to call him Orca. And he even started to act like one himself as he grew up, packed an weight, and brawled more than an Irish drunk.

"Rock," Orca acknowledged, standing up.

Orca stood 6 feet even and weighed 275 pounds. He had a large bandage on the right side of his forehead and his left eye was swollen.

Rock was enraged at what has happened to him and made it known. "As much as I preach for each of y'all to stay low, off the streets, let's take these drug crews' money from the shadows - the Dark Web- every now and then we have something or somebody who fucks wit one of us."

"And nobody fucks wit us," Chubb said coldly.

"Who did it?" Bhad Barbie asked in her little chipmunk voice. She was a nice looking brown skinned 16 year old with a round face and big titties. She had a small ass with a cute shape to it and she stood only five feet tall.

"Them Blood nyggaz did it," Orca told everyone. "I was on my way home from hangin' wit Chubb nem at the movies and them mufuckas followed me into the 7- Eleven and caught me at the soda rack. Four of 'em."

"For what?" Barbie wanted to know.

"Fuck for what," Rock ended the inquiry. "Don't matter for what. No one fucks with us."

"So whattawe gonna do?" Diamond Girl asked as she asked as she worked on a laptop. "Because we can inflict some pain on the fuckers from what I'm findin' in the MPD gang database."

"Whattoya mean?" Rock asked.

Diamond Girl was a thick white girl, 5 feet 5 inches tall, 17 years old, 195 founds, long blond hair and she stayed laced with same beautiful diamond jewelry most days out of the week. She was an excellent hacker.

"Mt. Vernon Police Department has a number of investigations going on," Diamond brought him the laptop. "They've identified banks where they keep money. We can ID theft those who are worth it and clean 'em out."

Rock shook his head. "Banks are not where they're keeping their real money."

Rock got up.

"Everybody that's here I need y'all to stay here," Chubb announced, looking at his watch.

Chubby left and was automatically followed out by Dojo, Shadow Warrior and Tommy Gunz. Obviously, the foul boys had already planned something because they knew exactly who was going. Of the four in their group Chubby was the youngest at 14 but looked older. Dojo was 18, light skinned and had dreads. He was tall and lanky. Shadow Warrior was also 18, brown skinned, wavvy hair, 5'9" and broad chested. He carried himself bigger than he actually was and was vicious in a fist fight. Tommy Gunz, was a shooter. He was skinny, couldn't fight, but he'd never run or cower either. He was 5 feet 10 inches tall with bad breath, loyal as hell to Rock. If Rock told him to kill he killed. At 18 he had a body count already that was up.

Something big was about to go down.

Chapter Eighteen

Savage Hoodz HQ
Mt. Vernon, NY

A little over an hour later three masked men jumped out of the white utility van with fully automatic versions of the MP5's draw on the couple smooching inside of the purple Sentra. A black girl named Rozetta yelped when the gunman at the driver's side bashed open the window sending glass spraying all over them.

"Fuck y'all fools want?!" the driver demanded.

"Out!" he was ordered.

When the man, D-Slice, complied he was immediately

subdued against the car, hands zip-tied behind his back, a black pillowcase thrown over his head and he was led to the white van.

"You wanna come?" the gunman asked the frightened passenger.

"No! Please no!" she shook her head.

He reached inside for her school backpack, opened it and dumped it all onto her lap.

"Aha! Rozetta McDunn, 143 Watson Avenue?" he asked. She nodded yes. "Get your shit outta this nygga car. Hurry! Pick it up!"

She did as she was instructed.

"Out!"

She got out of the car which was parked behind an abandoned bowling alley. Obviously, the couple had planned on some privacy for a little hanky panky after the gunman seen him pick the little cutie up after school at Mt. Vernon High School.

"This got nothing to do with you, Rozetta," the gunman, Tommy Gunz hissed. "This gangsta shit. Take yo lil ass home and you bet not even pray about this shit to god. Don't think. Don't say shit! Or else we gotchu. I gotcha ID. 143 Watson Avenue. Go!"

She didn't just "go" she *ran*.

Tommy Gunz jumped into the Nissan Sentra and followed the white van back

to HQ. On the way he threw Blood D-Slice's cellphone

out the window so it couldn't be

tracked out to the industrial section. Halfway there the van stopped and Tommy pulled

the Sentra into a quiet residential street and parked. The van pulled up and Shadow

Warrior handed him a red can filled with gasoline. The car's interior was doused with the liquid and Tommy stepped back to toss a match inside of it. The flames instantly

consumed the interior and Tommy jumped into the van.

Ten minutes later the van pulled up to their building and they led D-Slice in and up into the loft on the freight-style elevator. While they were absent everyone was doing their own thing. Whenever the elevator was moving everyone heard it or noticed the blinking red light above it.

The Savage Hood Girlz were all wearing masks and gloves as they packaged up an entire kilo of heroin entitled "5 Star." Anyone who used the 5-Star brand of heroin would not only get the highest they ever got, but that shit had to be taken with the Narcan nearby. The *VULKANIKACYD.onion* dark web site not only had the "5 star" heroin in its store but much more.

"Comin' up!" Rock yelled, turning the music down. "Comin' up!"

The elevator stopped and Sage opened the gate without being directed to. Out of

everyone who'd stayed behind Sage was the only one who knew the entire play aside from the boss.

"Orca!" Rock called him over.

Everyone was there now, curious as to who the person was with the hood on his head and zip-ties on his wrists.

"What da fuck?" Bhad Barbie said as she removed her latex gloves and threw them away.

"Sage," Rock tilted his head towards the hooded man after Tommy shoved him so hard he fell to the cement floor.

Sage bent down and snatched the black pillowcase off the head of the 18 year old light skinned member of the Blood gang.

Orca looked at him and nodded. "This one of them Almighty Black P. Stone nyggaz that jumped me. Aw man," Orca sighed and scratched his head.

"Take 'im to the showers," Rock ordered Dojo, Shadow, and Sage. While they did that Rock turned to Orca. "Whattaya mean 'aw man?' You nervous?"

Orca was honest. "Hell yeah. It's way more of them than us."

"You think so?" Rock shot back. "Son, we got soldiers all over. You just see whatchu see."

Orca scratched his head.

"Ain't no survival in bein' weak, son," Rock wisely told him. "Come on."

There was a line of shower stalls installed separate from the lofts four corner bathrooms. They had to enter the shower room through a set of double doors. To the right were sinks and mirror's where the men could stand in front of and shave.

And stools where the women could sit as if they were at a vanity and do their thing.

To the left were five separate private shower stalls. Tommy and several others took D-Slice inside of the first stall and Rock came in and used a hunting knife to cut all of his clothes off of him. Sage came in out of nowhere and produced a shiny new machete.

"Whattayu doing, Sage?" Juicy P asked him. She was the half black, half latina girlfriend of Ava Applez. Juicy was a bad little 16 year old bitch who, like Ava, was prolific at setting up and breaking down dark net firewalls. She was only 4 feet 11 inches and 100 pounds. Too bad she only liked pussy right now because Sage could tell she was getting dick curious by the way she flirted with him and tried to act like his "big sis" all the time. Sage could see through all that bull-shit. Her hot little ass wanted more than Ava's pretty choco-late face between them legs sucking all up on that "juicy" that Juicy P had in them panties.

Everyone was crowded in the shower room watching.

Rock looked down at the helpless, naked, D-Slice. "I need a plastic bag for all his clothes, shoes... where his phone at?"

"Threw it out the window so somebody can find it and use it," Tommy said.

"You faggot ass nyggas think Bugout for Blood Nimrod ever gonna letchu get away with this?!" Slice yelled more than asked.

"Fuck you Blood nyggas!" Rock snapped. "Y'all

remember them names. In fact, since knowledge is so powerful if you want to live ... how 'bout you give me more?"

"Fuck your mutha!" D-slice said and spit at Rock.

Rock smiled. "How y'all Bloods - and you ain't bleeding? Sage!"

Rock stepped on D-Slice's ankle. "I need one phone to tape this shit! Dojo, phone! And only Dojo!"

Sage stepped up with the machete and it was then that Juicy P and everyone else knew that this was all choreographed. Sage saw D-Slice's foot sticking out and Rock had it pinned down by the ankle Rock had all of his weight on it. Dojo had the cellphone filming D-Slice's wide eyed fear when he saw Sage with the gleaming machete in his black leather gloved hands.

"What the fuck?!" D-Slice was trying to stay brave but that machete had him ready to shit and Rock could tell. "W-whatchu gonna do with that?"

"We ain't gonna cut your long ass toenails wit it," Rock replied. "Give 'im a lil taste, son."

Sage pointed the razor sharp tip of the blade on D-Slice's scrotal sack and pulled the machete away from him. He almost breathed a sigh of relief but then, a delayed second in between, and he noticed that the blade had cut him wide open!

"Oh shit!" Diamond Girl whispered .

Juicy P moved closer to the action, watching Sage's swag more closely. All the girls wanted to see more.

"Aw! Oww! Shhhhh! Fucckkk you!" D-Slice shouted from the stinging pain. He kept looking down at the small stream and drip of blood. How he was scared.

"You gonna talk now?" Rock asked him.

Rock stood up and turned the hot water on.

"Sage," Rock said, still standing on his ankle. "Cut the fucking foot off!"

"*WAIT*!!!" D-Slice yelled. "Whattaya wanna know and do I walk outta here?"

"Taxi and a hundred dollar bill." Rock assured him. "Talk!"

Dojo recorded everything he told them about the Almighty Black P. Stone's Bronx and Mt. Vernon organization. He even mentioned P-Man, the highrise apartment up Hollow Park, Croton On The Hudson, members names, murders, drug spots and everything about Bugout, his capo, Blood Nimrod, and Lieutenant Blood Bain.

"You got it all Dojo?" Rock asked.

Dojo nodded. "Hell yeah."

Rock stepped away from D-Slice. "That it?" Rock asked his captive.

"Nimrod my bousin," D- Slice nodded. "He has me drive him everywhere. That's how I know everything," the young Blood member added.

"Aight," Rock stated. "We ain't gotta kill 'im. He can't go back now that he done went out bad. Get him something to wear, get 'im outta here."

"He lyin'," Sage suddenly spoke up. "Plus, what about avengin' the god, Orca? What about them jumpin' him?"

"I don't give a fuck if y'all rough 'im up," Rock stated walking off that'll even up the score."

Sage looked at Orca. "You want some?"

"Fuck that nygga, son," Orca, waved him off. "He prolly gon' go kill hisself somewhere."

Sage turned toward D-Slice who was smiling now. "Just do what the boss says nygga and gimme some clothes. Ya pussy ass man, Orca said-"

But Sage lost it after that. He swung the machete like he was swinging at a 90 mile per hour fastball and just like that he had done it! D-Slice's head had fallen off like a big onion that rolled off of the countertop inside of a ship's kitchen! As all of the women, except For Juicy P, screamed and ran to get Rock, Sage just continued on chopping at the nygga as if he was prime beef or a pig corpse! Juicy P recorded everything, even the beheading.

Rock returned and made everyone stand back because blood was flying everywhere.

"You gonna stop him?" Barbie asked Rock.

"For what?" Rock shrugged. "If y'all came from where that young man came from..."

He let it hang.

Sage had chopped D-Slice up limb from limb. Arms, legs, torso... that machete was

lethal and powerful. When he was done he stood there

breathing mad, hard, and sweating. He cut the water off, looked at the bloody walls in the aluminum stall... then turned to his gang.

"Why'd you do all that?" Chubb asked him, shaken at the brutality of it all.

"Maaan, let him do what - " Rock stopped his brother but Sage stopped Rock.

First, though, he stepped up to Juicy P with his hand out. She reluctantly gave him her cellphone. He took out the SIM card and gave her the phone back.

"Nah, Rock, I'll tell 'i'm why," Sage said trying to wipe some of the blood off of his face. "How in the fuck are we Savage Hoodz when we do nothin' savage?"

"He right," Tommy Gunz said. "But so you know, nygga, you ain't the only one wit a body count in here. But you right. And *wrong*, mufucka cuz we'll kill any mufucka and have. But animals like this, he got what he deserved fuckin wit us. Nobody fucks wit us. And we need to mean that shit."

Rock stepped in. "Save them graduation speeches and let's get this maggot chopped up real good so we can burn him and dump his ashes in the ocean. Sage jump yo happy ass in the shower and get that blood off ya. Everybody that was standing here bag ya clothes. Trust me there's blood spatter on 'em. We gotta hit these stalls, walls, floors, and ceiling wit the bleach and ammonia in the power washer."

Sage said nothing more.

Chapter Nineteen

Savage Hoodz HQ
Mt. Vernon, NY

"Oh shit!" Juicy P exclaimed and turned her head for a second but she couldn't help but turn back and look as she handed Sage a towel, under clothes and a sweatsuit. "I didn't mean to... um... you know."

But she was meaning to look and got an eyeful because Sage was not just already half hard, he really had a body that made girls mouth's water. And though he was young he already looked 14 and he was way ahead of his time on how minds worked.

"I know you wit a girl but you be thinking of me when she lickin' that pretty little pussy you got," he accused her. "Tell da truth."

"Ew, no I don't!" she shook her head. "I been wit girls only, since I was eleven."

"Look how good I look," he teased, his dick at full staff now. "I'm telling you I'd eat that pussy like Mr. Porno and let you ride till you squirt."

"You are so nasty," she said backing up as he walked towards her. "What are you doing?"

"C'mere," he said softly.

She stopped and he came up to her.

He never hesitated. He reached under her short denim skirt and rubbed her pussy through her thong panties.

"Ooouuu, no, stoooop," she whispered. "We can't just."

"You like a man touchin' you," he said in her ear. "Now your turn..."

"Whaaaat?" she whined as he placed her small hand around his hot meat. "It's so hard."

"Because of how fuckin' horny you make it," he said humping her hand. "Real fast..."

He pulled her into the last shower stall and closed the door.

"No!" she protested weakly.

"Just kiss it," he begged her. His dick was throbbing like crazy.

"It's squirting," she said as she tumbled down to her knees.

"When it loves someone that happens," he explained. "Go ahead... I know you seen the Internet porn. Suck that dick baby."

She kissed him all around first and then sucked him in two, then three, four and five inches, instantly adoring the taste and texture of male. He held her head and started fucking her mouth in earnest. Not wanting to get caught he hurried up and bussed a nut in her mouth. She wanted her first taste of cum and she did all she could to suck it up and swallow all of it. Some dribbled out on her chin, but she got most of it.

She stood up and got ready to run when he caught her. "Wait!"

"Huhn?" she said. He dropped to his knees and pulled her black thong panties down. He kissed her small "V" and stuck his tongue out to taste her juices. Man was she soaked!

He stood up. "You still a virgin?"

She shook her head no. "Ava took it with a strap on dildo."

"She gotta share this pussy okay?"

She looked at him for one moment. "I haveta go!"

And with that she scurried out of the showers.

He smiled after she left.

The boys were out in the back of the building burning D-Slicks body parts in a 55-gallon steel drum. Sage got dressed and used the power washer to clean the showers out with a strong solution of bleach, ammonia and soap which washed all evidence of a crime down the drain.

"C'mere lil nygga," Rock hollered at him once everything was done.

They were all back in the living room, seated all around again. This time Rock came up to Sage with a see through double Ziploc bag of ashes and handed it to him.

"You gotta take yo young ass home before Miss Maria start trippin'," Rock warned him. "Youse a crazy coldhearted, mufucka you know that?"

"Thatta be a good moniker for him," Tommy Gunz said. "Just throwin' it out there. COLDHEARTED, one whole word."

"You ever show everybody those videos of your supposed dad...?" Rock asked him.

"They hackers," Sage told him. "They prolly seen everything."

Sage took out his phone after sitting the Ziploc bag on the floor.

"Set it up on the big screen," Rock told him.

He plugged his phone up to the XBOX and a minute later he played the Big Kato video followed by multiple snippets of news program coverage, and newspaper clips of what had happened. He even had a clip of the fire and deaths of Daphne and Armand.

Some of the girls were crying.

"A lot of y'all ain't know that bout the lil homie," Rock

stated as he turned the big screen off. "Now y'all know and he'll defend Savage Hoodz to the death."

"I always gotcha back, Coldhearted," Tommy swore as he embraced him.

Chubb nodded. "You already know. Me, too."

"Definitely got my respect," Rock declared.

Barbie kissed his check. "Me, too, baby bro."

Literally every single Savage Hoodz male and female in the room showed him love. And called him no more Sage but COLDHEARTED.

"Chubb I gotta drop you off before madukes trips," Rock warned him. "Grab that Ziploc, son, so we can dump that shit in the river along the way. It still got pieces of teeth and bone in it."

Sage had made his mark among his crew as well as in the streets and at school. And now he'd even earned the hardcore nickname: *Coldhearted.*

But, as life would teach him, his heart was about to be forced to become even colder.

Part Two

Heartless

Quote

Sometimes I am God,
If I say a man dies,
He dies that same day.
- Pablo Escobar

Chapter Twenty

The Warrant Search
Mt, Vernon, NY
Saturday 11:00 AM

On his 14th birthday Maria wanted to throw a huge birthday party for Coldhearted at their Mt. Vernon home and invite all of their family members and friends from the kids' school. As she was discussing this with Papo the police showed up with a warrant to search the house.

It was 11:00 AM Saturday so the cops caught everyone at home. It was a beautiful April day, sunny and clear, out, and this intrusion not only surprised Papo and Maria it angered them.

"What's this about, officer?" Maria demanded as ten officials showed up at the residence. One of them had on a DEA jacket and another one wore an FBI jacket. "And why are *they* here?"

"I'm Corporal Ben Haines, ma'am," the skinny, clean cut white man stated. He gave her a copy of the warrant. "Where is the room Sage Michael Garcia-Daniels AKA Coldhearted sleeps?"

Maria stared at Coldhearted with angry slitted eyes and pointed left. As the officers began their search there she turned on Coldhearted. "What'd you do now?"

"Turned Blacker?" he stated sarcastically.

"Boy don't you get smart wit me!" Maria warned him as she sat next to Papo in the living room.

Lilly sat next to her brother on the sofa. She laid her head against his arm and he pulled the beautiful 9 year old's back up against him and stroked her long black tresses.

"Sage what's this?" Papo pointed at the warrant and the presence of the Feds. "It says here you're part of a online identity theft ring... and y'all are suspected of purchasing weapons?"

Coldhearted shut down. He knew it was some bullshit involved.

"Now ain't the time to go silent!" Papo snapped.

"Maybe it is, Papo." Maria sat with her legs crossed bouncing her foot up and down like a pit and a pendulum.

Over the past year the Savage Hoodz were able to use the information D-Slice had given them and steal tens of thousands of dollars from Bugout's Almighty Black P. Stones. They had also went after the more powerful Bloods in Brooklyn led by P-Man where the take was even larger: $200,000. But that was nothing. Using their social security numbers, birth certificates, drivers licenses and other documents Savage Hoods stole the identities of every individual Blood member they could identify in both sects. These included Bugout, Blood Nimrod, Blood Bain, forty other northern Bronx and Mt. Vernon Bloods and P-Man with eighteen of his closest affiliates in Brooklyn.

Savage Hoodz opened up credit lines, and bank accounts and they used them to purchase nearly a million dollars in Bitcoin over the dark net, And they spent all of the Bitcoin on building up their massive dark net superstore *VULKANIKA-CYD.onion*.

Maria watched the police officers, remove several boxes containing books, harddrives, and flashdrives from Coldhearted's room. But ultimately no weapons or anything pointing to his involvement in an identity theft ring. Maria and Papo were told that the digital equipment would be forensically analyzed and if it contained no evidence of crime it would be returned.

"I wish you were old enough," Maria told Coldhearted

after the authorities left. "Or I'd put your ass out on the street!"

Coldhearted just ignored her and that pissed her off even more. Papo tried to get her to calm down.

"Just leave him," Papo said it in Spanish. But he was careful because Sage understood Spanish. They all spoke Spanish to him. Even Lilly who was half black half Puerto Rican spoke to him in Spanish which she mostly learned from her mother when she'd been alive.

But she followed him to his room. "You think you're grown! But you gonna learn the hard way! I'm tired of it! I'm about to have you placed in a boy's home or somethin' because I can't have this in my house! Around Lilly!"

"It's not your house," Coldhearted reminded her.

"What did you say boy?" She said it like he'd spit it into her ear.

He stood up to her in his room as Papo came to the door Lilith sat on his bed behind him.

"Here's what I said," Coldhearted stated. *"This is not your house.* This is me and Lilly's house. You think I don't understand that?"

"You better watch your mouth, *hijo*," Papo warned him.

"Tell her that," Coldhearted shot back. "Ain't nobody kickin' me out of my house. Or puttin' me in no group or foster home."

"You've lost your mind!" Maria yelled at him.

Coldhearted sat next to Lilly and left it at that.

Papo pulled Maria out of the room.

Lilly wasn't dumb either. "Now she's mad. Are they gonna try to send, you away?" she asked.

Coldhearted shook his head no. "Ain't nobody doin' nothin'. I won't let no one take you from me. You my baby always right?"

Lilly nodded and hugged him. "Forever."

He opened his laptop and pulled up a new online banking app he'd had established for himself with Rock's assistance. "Look, mami," he said to Lilly.

"Oou is that our Money?" she asked him.

"Not the money in our trust," he shook his head. "This is the money I made with my crew. But yeah, it's both of ours. Let's call it back-up money, okay?"

She nodded.

He emailed a picture of his account balance to Maria and Papo just in case they were getting any bright ideas. In fact. he wrote: "*#LawyerMoney*," and he emailed that, too.

"You go 'head and enjoy ya day, mama," he said and kissed his baby sister on her lips.

She sauntered on out of his room.

He showered, dressed and walked past Maria and Papo on his way out.

Chapter Twenty-One

Riccardi New & Used Cars
Queens NY
10:00 AM

Coldhearted and Liza cruised at 60 mph down the Bronx-Queens-Expressway until Liza hit the Van Wyck Expressway in a green Town & Country minivan rental car. They were on their way to Riccardi New Used & Cars. On the way there they shared a blunt of some exotic Kush.

Sixteen years old now Liza had filled out in the hips, thighs and ass more but she still stayed small up top. Coldhearted was nuts about her and she felt the same about him.

"I heard they searched the house," Liza said, turning the Sirius Satellite radio down.

He nodded. "Yeah... don't miss the exit, stupid."

"Shut up," she giggled, high as shit. She exited on Hillside Avenue and drove straight up the road until they saw Parsons Boulevard.

"They searched but whatn't nuttin' there to find," he told her.

"You must be into some heavy shit," she commented.

"Not really," he said pointing. "That it over there?"

She made a right into the car dealership parking lot and found a place to park in the far left corner of the lot.

"What made you pick this spot?" he asked her.

"My mom bought her car from here," she said. "I can't believe we even sitting here about to buy a car."

"You need to teach me to drive," he said as she leaned over to kiss him. "Don't I teach you everything?" she teased, rubbing his crotch.

"Mm, and I don't take the wheel afterwards?" He was hardening under her touch.

She smiled at his comment. "Since I was twelve and you was ten in that closet."

He laughed and pushed her hand away. "You making it hard. C'mon, *chica*."

They walked around the car lot until they were met by a female salesperson.

"First car?" she guessed.

Liza giggled, still high. "For both of us."

"You're a couple?" she asked. "I mean you're buying a car to share?"

"Something like that," Liza said, unsure.

"Well I'm Alena Parks, " she introduced herself. "So, we're looking for something used, new, financed?"

Coldhearted pulled several stacks of brand new one hundred dollar bills out of his pants pocket. "I just wanna get somethin' fast and furious for me and my honey here. New I hope, right mami?"

Liza took the money, leafed through it, and put it securely inside of her purse. "Daddy you should've showed me all of that... Miss Parks, you see we don't need no tax trouble. We have the cash for a new car but can't prove how we make the money."

"Girl, please," the saleswoman waved her off. "We get rappers and hustlers coming in here all the time. Box is just trying to move inventory."

"Box?" Liza looked puzzled.

"Mr. Box we call him because his head is shaped like a box," Alena said. "And he's named Mr. Boxman."

Liza laughed. "He owns it?"

Coldhearted walked off and checked out a white BMW M1 Competition. It was priced at $40,113 with low miles, certified used. Liza watched him and realized in that moment that she no longer had a boy but a man. A very young man but a man nonetheless.

She checked out the BMW and salivated. She knew then that he came to *buy*.

"Wish you had this in charcoal black with the ghost finish," he said.

They got inside of a Porsche next but it was priced out of range.

"Papi, I like this one," he heard her call out from down the lot about six cars up from where he was.

He walked up to where Alena and Liza stood and saw that they were standing next to a charcoal black Cadillac Escalade with the ghost finish. He had to smile at the look on Liza's face.

He hopped inside of it and loved it if Liza did.

"Let me get the keys," Alena said and walked off.

"Where's this cash comin' from, Daddy?" Liza demanded. "And don't say your trust cuz my mom and Maria been talkin'. She tryna get you locked up."

"Maria is?" Coldhearted frowned.

Liza nodded. "Her and my moms was on the phone for hours yesterday about you and them cops comin' to search. Something about a school email?"

Coldhearted nodded. "One of the emails at school a dozen mufuckas use was linked to the theft of tens of thousands of Westchester County student's identities being stolen... well, their personal info being stolen. Other emails being hacked. Including teachers, staff, board of education members, you name it my crew got their info."

"Crew?" she asked. "You have a crew? Not just Rock and Chubb?"

He shook his head. "Let's cop this truck, mami. I'll tell you what's up."

"What about this weapon deal they had on the warrant?" She asked, worriedly. "Guns they said."

"There was a purchase made and they can't find it," he shrugged. "You know how school shootings and all that is. My crib aint the only one they hit. They hit six others. Chubb's, too."

"So, they want them guns," Liza stated shaking her head. "You might as well live in my neighborhood. Guns going off every day, cops buggin', killin' Latino nyggas, Black nyggas. And you up in the suburbs, bein' searched by Feds, you better watch Maria and Papo."

"Me and you, 'bout to get our own crib," he mentioned. "I want you wit me."

Alena returned.

"Are you serious?!" Liza asked, her mouth all open.

"Fuckin' right I'm serious," Sage stated. "I love you. You my mami right?"

"Yeah. I swear it," she told hm and they kissed.

Liza was the one with the driver's license so she was the authorized driver, they fell in love with the vehicle and thirty minutes later were back at the dealership following a test drive.

Lenny Boxman was a skinny 45 year old Jewish car dealer with black curly hair and silver, wire rimmed, eyeglasses on his clean shaven face. Alena brought him into her office and he shook their hands.

"That Caddy is top notch, forty six grand is the lowest I can go on a cash deal," he said. "And youse only have thirty eight."

Coldhearted had an envelope on him which he gave to Liza. She gave Box another

eight grand out of the envelope.

"You have another five we can make the IRS worries disappear," he added.

Liza counted out the $5000. "How?"

"We finance it or make it look that way," he shrugged. "But not through a bank. Through us. Since you've paid in full we'll give you monthly pay slips. Each month you mail in a blank slip and we'll handle the rest. Just put your title up safe. It's yours. And at the end of the day you'll also build up a fantastic credit profile."

"Both of our names?" she demanded.

"Are you nuts?" Box asked. "Trust me. He's too young, you're barely legal. And if you ever, wanna trade it, come on back and we'll upgrade it, do all the custom work, etcetera. Okay?"

He was a fast talker.

Liza and Coldhearted sat through a lot of paper signing

but were back on the road in no time. They abandoned the rental van and Liza told the rental agency where it had "broken down" at.

Chapter Twenty-Two

Liza's Pregnancy
Queens DMV
1:00 PM

He started from the beginning and told her almost everything.

"My crew is Savage Hoodz and Savage Hood Girlz," he started as they sat at the Queens DMV on Jamaica Avenue to get license plates for the truck. "We operate one of

the biggest illegal superstores on the dark net."

"Dark net, dark net," she wondered out loud. "I heard of child porn on there."

"Man, if me and you make a porn and put it on the dark web that's child porn," he said. "So, we ain't alarmed about that shit. We careful 'bout our porn - we don't have no toddlers on it. Anyway, we have all the best coke, heroin, molly, Percoset, zannies, K2, K2 liquid, weed, weed products, ghost guns, guns, and way more. ID theft is our biggest moneymaker."

He spoke for twenty minutes straight.

She slapped his arm. "So, these Savage Hood Girlz... when y'all bring 'em in y'all gang y'all bang em?"

"Huhn? You buggin'!" he laughed. "Nah. And no I ain't fuck none of 'em though this one lesbian girl."

"Lesbian girl what?" Liza, asked to see if he'd be honest with her.

"She told me she only been wit girls since she was eleven," he said. "I just wanted to see if I could get her to betray her girl Ava Applez."

"Did she?"

He nodded. "She sucked me off in the showers and I kissed and tasted her pussy."

"Is that what we gonna do?" Liza asked him.

He looked at her. "No ... I mean my dick be wantin' to but I don't be going after girls. I mean... I love you and we supposed to be cousins but that's adoption. Look. I'm brown. You white."

"I'm Boriqua and Dominicana," she corrected him. "I'm just white skin but just as Black as you. And I don't care if you my cousin. That makes the sex even hotter. But I wanna be the only bitch."

"So, you ain't have other boys?" he asked her. "I mean, I thought -"

"Only thing I ever did I told you," she said. "I had oral sex with several boys. That's how I did it so good with you. And I almost let a boy take my virginity but he bussed before he could finish. If you want just one loyal wifey that's me. Nobody gonna hold you down like me."

"You a woman now," he said, expressing a vulnerable insecurity about himself he'd never show to any other person, male or female. "I'm fourteen so I'd believe you'll always find someone else. A grown man."

He almost made her cry.

"I'm pregnant with your baby, Papi," she revealed, a tear escaping from her left eye despite her efforts to control her emotions.

He turned to her on the wooden bench they sat on. "You kidding me?"

She shook her head no, her nose and ears turned red. She couldn't hold back the tears this time. "I wouldn't play about no shit like that," she looked at him.

He dried her eyes "You sad?"

"No. Yes ...." Then she shrugged. "I'm only sixteen. You sayin' I'm a woman. I'm still a girl you worrying about me leaving you and I'm worrying about you leaving me."

He hugged her to him and held her tightly. "You my baby. You and Lilly."

Liza smiled at hearing that.

He kissed her several times, smelling her sweetness and running his hands all through her long luxurious tresses.

"So Imma be a Daddy?"

"You already my Daddy, baby," she said as her number was called. "So, about this moving in ... me and my mom fight so much and she always threatening to throw me out."

They paid the fees for the license plates and registration and exited. They attached the stickers and put the plates on and took a selfie in front of the Cadillac. "Happy Birthday Daddy you 'bout to be a father!" she gushed.

They drove to Savage Hoodz Hangout which was another loft not even a mile away from HQ. It was converted into a loft living quarters by construction crews that came in and did the miraculous transformation to the former boathouse.

The difference in the Hangout was that the owners had converted the entire building into six luxury lofts, private parking, laundry, free maintenance, utilities were separate.

They parked and went up to the fourth floor where the biggest of all the lofts Were. Coldhearted let them in by unlocking the elevator gate which told him no one else was there. It was a far cry from all the luxuries SHZ-HQ had but it was still nice and part his.

Everyone in the organization were paid "dividends" each

week based on the profits. However, each member was aware that VULKANIKACYD was an illegal underground corporation that they all owned and were employed by. And part of the profits they were all due went back into building up the corporation. In many instances it wasn't even the narcotics and weapons that sent the corporation soaring but the millions of identities they stole and then resold to VULKANIKACYD buyers and subscribers.

After making love to his bombshell girlfriend they lay nude in his room talking about all of this.

"Then why ever sell the illegal stuff," she asked naively.

"Huhn?"

She laughed. "I mean the narcotics and weapons. You know that weed got me."

"The power," he answered. "That's what Rock said. And about you smokin' and drinkin'."

She turned over onto her back. "I wanted to quit as soon as I found out but was thinking you wouldn't want this baby. Then today... seein' you react like you did. I just know you gonna go all out protecting us and makin' us a family."

"I want Papo and Maria outta my house," he told her. "And I want Lilly cuz half is hers."

"How much is that place?" Liza quizzed.

"The original was $350k plus," he recalled. "Insurance paid for that and she kept an additional $100K of our trust to add more to the original. And there's a mortgage involved."

"Whatchu gonna do?"

"I don't wanna tell you that," he said. "Is the smokin' and drinkin' done?"

"I promise." She lay on top of him. "Don't kill 'em though okay?"

He stared up at her "Now I promise."

"So, you want this baby?" she asked as he stroked her hair out of her face.

He nodded yes. "You know my background. I showed you all the videos and news clips. I want and need this baby. I want and need a bad bitch like you as my wife and best friend."

"You really know I have yo back, she said, kissing him more hungrily than ever now, the love deeper and different now that his seed was rooted inside of her. "I love you so much." She reached between them and inserted his hardened length inside of her.

"I love you, too, Liza..."

Chapter Twenty-Three

"C'mere for a minute, Sage," Papo called out to him when he walked into the house with Liza behind him.

Papo was looking out into the driveway at the new Cadillac through the kitchen windows.

"W'sup?" Coldhearted asked.

Liza didn't stick around. She went off to find Lilly. Papo sat at the kitchen table and motioned for Coldhearted to take a seat.

"I see from that bank statement you sent us that you into something big," Papo stated slowly, choosing his words cautiously.

"I'm not the first teenager to make his own money," Coldhearted said. "I learned when I was a baby not to trust parents and guardians and people that think they hold power over you."

Papo took a deep breath. "Well, something's gone real cold in you. You are just bad. Through and through. So, what Maria and I decided is to allow you to live out on your own and we'll handle all your bills- *responsibly* - through your trust. And as long as you stay in school and graduate she'll get off of the trust on your eighteenth birthday. As far as this house goes Lilly has nine years before she turns eighteen so this is where she'll be. If you wanna visit, then come visit. But you have a few days to find somewhere else to live."

Liza and Lilly were standing there to hear the end of what Papo said. Lilly was visibly upset with what she'd heard but Coldhearted led her to his room.

"Hey what'd I tell you?" he whispered to her.

She was close to tears. "That you'd never let no one take me away from you."

"Or me from you. We *always*."

"And forever," she completed their special saying.

"Well," he put his hands on his hips. "Why the fuckin' tears?"

She wiped her eyes, laughing at the funny way he was standing.

"Good girl."

Late That Night

PAPO AND MARIA were at home asleep late that night when they were forcefully removed out of the bed. Maria screamed and it was heard by Lilly who was in the bed next to her brother.

"Shh, mami, it's okay, shh," he whispered to her "Hold onto me. I promise it's okay."

Dark hoods were placed over both of Maria and Papo's heads by Savage Hoodz

goons: Shadow Warrior, Choir Boy, Wolfman, Orca, Tommy Gunz, HK and Mac-11. Their mouths were gagged so they couldn't yell for help. Their eyes were blindfolded. Large headphones blaring loud rock and roll music were placed over their ears to torture them. With the addition of the black hoods, they were totally disoriented as they were carried out to a white van in the attached garage.

The Savage Hood Girlz transported them from there to a Bronx house on 233rd and Laconia Avenue. There the couple was separated and shoved into two different rooms where their gags were removed but the hoods and loud head-phones were left in place.

Back at the Mt. Vernon house, Coldhearted was all alone with Lilly. The Hoodz had already exited.

"C'mere, mami," Coldhearted urged Lilly.

She put on her bathrobe and Dora The Explorer slippers and they walked into Maria and Papo's room. She was confused. The bed was nicely made, it was all straightened out, no sign of a struggle.

"Where are they?" Lilly asked him. "I thought I heard something happen."

"Nah, they was fightin'," he lied. "And then they left."

"Oh," she said yawning.

Lilly went back to bed.

The following morning a moving truck came and all of their things were packed and removed. Liza arrived later in the day to watch Lilly.

"Whatchu do?" she asked him as he hopped into the Porsche that Rock picked him up in.

"I'll holla at you," was all he said and Rock peeled off.

The Bronx House

233rd & Laconia

Bronx, NY

. . .

Forty-five minutes later he was snatching the hood, headphones and blindfold off of Maria. When she was able to get her bearings she could see that she was in a large empty bedroom with wooden floors.

"Where am I, where's Papo?" she asked, taking deep breaths after being gagged all night.

Standing in the room with them were four hoodied and masked figures holding guns. Her teeth started to chatter out of fear. Coldhearted stared at her and opened up a laptop that he knew she recognized.

"You, Maria Garcia, are inside of a bedroom of your new house," he explained. "Papo is in another room. Do you ever want to see um again?"

"Look, Sage, whatever you're trying-"

"I ASKED YOU A QUESTION!" he exploded in her face.

"Yes!" She jumped, closing her eyes tightly.

He sat back down in the chair he'd been sitting on and he opened up the laptop. "Here's what you're going to do. You're goin' to access the bank's website and request that my trust money be transferred into my savings account, dissolving the trust. And the bank will text or email you a code to ensure that it is you who is makin' the request."

Tommy Gunz cut the restraints from her hands and Coldhearted placed the laptop onto her lap.

"Where's Heartless?" he asked.

Choir Boy produced his razor sharp machete which he placed across his lap. Maria saw it and her own heart dropped into her stomach. He watched closely as she typed the request into the banks online system. When she paused, Coldhearted pressed the tip of the pointed blade sharply into her side.

"I have your phone," he said, when the bank sent her a six-digit code. He took the laptop and sent the code back to the bank himself. Moments later they wanted a copy of Maria's driver's license which he took a picture of and sent it to the link the bank provided. A few minutes later the process was complete.

"Now, Lilly," Coldhearted demanded. "She has a savings account, too. Do it!"

"You need to think about her future!" Maria pleaded with him. "Sage, please."

Sage used his phone to pull up an encrypted video he had buried on the dark web. Once he found it he showed it to her. "Watch it!" He ordered her.

What she saw sickened and struck a fear in her that she'd never even imagined. It was of Coldhearted using his machete - named "Heartless"- to kill, decapitate and chop to pieces D-Slick.

"Ain't no Sage no more, Maria," he told her. "Just Cold-hearted. Now... *do it!*"

She didn't pause or hesitate a second longer. She had

Lilly's trust money transferred into her savings account held at the same bank.

"By the way," Coldhearted started but stopped. "Go get Papo and the others. Moments passed before Papo was shoved into the room, blindfold removed with the rock music and gag. He also had his constraints cut loose...

"Maria!" he cried, hugging her. "Mami!"

Coldhearted slapped the shit out of him. "Ayo - *fuck her*!! You listen to me!! This is your new home! No more Mt. Vernon! No more Lilly! No more livin' off our trust! Your cars are parked outside. Movers brought all your things here. And, just so you know, we hacked all of your records and I see where you somehow embezzled over thirty thousand dollars from our trust funds and deposited it in a bank in the Dominican Republic."

"No, we didn't!" Maria protested.

Coldhearted stood up "You did because I say you did. And because the FBI will be told that you did and I have the proof. Call it *severance pay!*"

Maria and Papo shook their heads.

"C'mon gang," Coldhearted began to, walk out. "Ah, almost forgot. Liza is pregnant. I'm gonna be a Dad!"

He laughed on his way out.

Tommy Gunz cut and removed the rest of Maria's constraints, gag, headphones and blindfold. He put them inside of a trash bag along with Papo's.

"Well, look at it this way," Tommy told them. "You have

your lives *and* his thirty grand in your D.R. accounts. You can thank Liza for him not takin' that machete to youse."

"All of you are monsters," Maria said, shaken.

Tommy Gunz nodded and they all disappeared from the house...

Chapter Twenty-Four

Coldhearted hired Family Law Attorney Melissa Verducci from Mt. Vernon and she met with him, Lilly, Liza, and Tanya Taylor - Rock and Chubb's mother. Tanya accepted the role of temporary guardian over Coldhearted and Lilly to protect them from being taken into custody by the Department of Social Services.

"That's all I want, all I need, Ms. Taylor," he told her. "I got it from here until the next court date."

Liza moved in with him despite all Elizabeth had warned her about regarding what Maria and Papo had told her and the rest of the Garcia family, about what he had done to them.

"*Hija*, that boy is a monster," Elizabeth had pleaded with her daughter as she was backing up to leave.

"I'm pregnant with his baby, mama," Liza had pleaded. "I *love* him. I've loved him since I was twelve!"

"Sweetie," her mom had said. "He's a gangster. He had your *blood* abducted from her sleep! And he showed them a video of him decapitating a man and chopping up his body!"

"That's not real!" Liza had countered. "Did they tell you they stole money from his and Lilly's trust accounts? And they were tryna muscle him out of his trust and his house? Mama why every time's money involved people lose their minds?"

Elizabeth, seeing she'd been fighting a losing battle with her daughter, had given up. "Okay, *mija*. Go. But ask him about chopping up the man. Ask to see the video. And when you see it send it to the police."

The evening he had come from Ms. Taylor's house after the Temporary Guardianship hearing had been concluded, Liza, Lilly and Coldhearted had eaten and were in bed when Liza asked him the burning question.

"You ever kill somebody?" She searched his face for lies.

There were no lies. "Maria told your mom what she saw." Liza nodded.

"That's how I got my nickname," he admitted.

"Can I see it?" she asked him.

He looked at Lilly. She was knocked out on the bed between them.

"Why?"

Liza shrugged. "I don't know it's scary to think about but strangely exciting if that makes sense?"

They left Lilly in her bed and went to his bed where he accessed the video from the dark web. She watched it with an intensity in her eyes. When it was over she handed him the phone back.

"Delete it," she commanded him.

"Why? It's safe where it is," he protested.

She shook her head. "Unh, unh. Delete it."

He shrugged. He wiped it clean and destroyed the encryption code, too. "Gone." But it really wasn't.

"I don't want nothing out there that can come back and harm my baby boy," she said, kissing him. "That gangster shit my mom don't understand but I do. And look..."

She took his hand and placed it into her people purple satin panties. She was wetter than bathwater.

He pushed her backward and removed her underwear. Leaving them dangling off of her left ankle. "The video made you this wet?"

"I told you," she said as he mashed his face into her wet mango.

"Damn you mad juicy." He licked his lips, her moisture all over his nose and chin. She smelled almost like fresh fruit juice against his skin.

She pulled her legs back and let him have all he wanted of her. He caught her salty sweet, little clitoris between his lips and lightly sucked on it, letting his wet tongue do twists around it. He had learned to tease her by not paying it 100% attention. In between well-timed moments he would stop to pull the skin back off of the clit and he would blow on it. Then his tongue would trace circles all around her vulva, kissing her soft white skin affectionately.

"Liza you smell so fresh, baby," he told her and held her ass and waist as he rubbed his nose all in and around her pussy.

"Oh god!" her beautiful moans came and turned him on as she squeezed her small breasts and pulled and pinches her pencil eraser like nipples.

He couldn't get intimate enough with this bombshell Latina. He pushed her knees back until they were on the sides of her head. He started to lightly kiss her asshole and lick all around it and inside of it. She pushed him away and he licked his lips as if they'd lost something.

"I got you, Papi," she said and flipped over onto her stomach. "When I masturbate I turn like this and fuck my pussy with one hand while reaching back and fingering my ass with the other... wishing your tongue was in me. Don't be shy, Daddy, please, please put your face and tongue all in that ass."

The way she spoke had him hard as hell, fucking the sheet as he did as she told him to do. She had no problem teaching him and demanding what she wanted. She loved controlling him, the sex.

"Oooh, fuuuuccckk!" She shouted as squirts of her cream bussed into his mouth. He was eating the asshole and catching all of her cream. "You swallowin' it aintchu, Daddy? You catchin' that cum huhn?"

He nodded and held her hand as she backed into his sweet brown face. He held her asscheeks apart and had his face buried in her as if she was whipcream pie. His two fingers were inside of her now, one hand holding her ass down as she screamed into the pillow, galloping into several small orgasms.

"Oh, fuck. Oh, fuck. Oh Fuck." She turned over, fainting hard. "I wanna suck your dick and drink your cum, Daddy."

But, instead, he just kissed her, deep. So deep. As if they had just gotten married... Or as though they were saying goodbye. He gathered her up in his arms and held her tight, whispering over and over again, "I love you, mami. I love that you havin' my baby... I love the baby already."

She spooned against him, loving that he was only wanting to hold her and be affectionate. He wrapped his arms around her naked body, clutching his hands on her belly, kissing her back, shoulders and neck. She held onto his arms and caressed them.

Soon, they drifted off to sleep...

Chapter Twenty-Five

P-Man Pops Up
Croton in The Hudson Apts.

In Hollow Park, in their Croton On The Hudson highrise, there was a highstakes meeting going on between Bugout, Blood Nimrod, Blood Bain, and the notorious Blood P-Man. They were seated in the luxurious living room, involved in a heated discussion over what should be done about the money they were losing from the northern Bronx and south Mt. Vernon area.

"You told us to find out who was fuckin' up our bottom line and I think we did that," Bain was saying, nearly shouting. "But when we load up to lay these maggots out-"

"I told him not to go after them nyggas," P-Man admitted. "First off it was assumption that we was goin' on. Second, they school kids!"

P-Man was 6 feet 1 inches tall, a visibly in-shape muscular build, brown skinned, big nose, big lips and dark brown eyes that were set deep into his face. As soon as he started talking one could hear that West Coast Los Angeles accent drip from his authoritative voice. Though he now operated from out of Brooklyn, he still had a crew of Bloods getting money from out of Chicago and in L.A. The Almighty Black P. Stones were a strong and ruthless network under him.

"We start shootin' school kids in the suburbs even if they all Black and doin' crime, the FBI will still villify us," P. Man stated wisely. "And what if the investigator is pointin' the finger in a fishbowl?"

Nimrod was still steaming. "They hacked into my email, my girl email, cleaned out our savings, and did the same to everyone in this room!"

"*Dozens* of my people," Bugout vouched.

P-Man stopped them. "This is the epicenter of everything. Your quote unquote missin' man just ups and disappears and not long afterwards we all of a sudden get our identities stolen? That's also why I said to pause. Did he walk off with a phone, or laptop, with all of our personal information and sell Blood business to hackers?"

"D-Slick was loyal," Bugout said.

"Money can change loyalty," P-Man told him. "I want eyes on Mt. Vernon High School. Let's see if we can see which kids are standing out the most, what they're pullin' up in, what they're spendin' money on, and so forth."

"Anyone ever hear of VULKANIKACYD?" Taizhan's sultry voice interjected from the desk she was quietly occupying as the men spoke.

They couldn't see her face because she was sitting behind where the giant, curved, 79-inch HDTV sat on a marble stand, blocking the desk behind it.

"What's that?" P-Man asked.

"I've heard of it," Nimrod said. "It's a dark net site. It's hell to get into unless you have the right software and codes another member has to walk you through to get onto it."

Taizhan put it up on the 79- inch smart screen. "My girlfriend's guy told her how he's been getting' his ocran sent to him at a dropbox in New Rochelle. He orders it, pays in Bitcoin, and it's their overnight delivery. He thinks the VULKANIKACYD owners are in Westhester."

Bugout responded first. "I know shit about the dark net but what I do know is it is extremely secretive. So, how's dude know the owners are in Westchester County, and so what?"

She shrugged. "I don't know. But he was in a chat room going back and forth with an employee of VULKANIKACYD and although they have you believe they're in North Korea, Taiwan, or somewhere, the employee gave my girl's guy *exact* directions to a safe dropbox location in New

Ro. I mean how would you know that unless you been there? Sure, you can google, 'dropboxes' I guess but the really discreet ones?"

"It might be somethin'," P-Man said. "But what? They movin' on the dark net that's the dark net. Anyhow let's hunt the hackers who took our money, and caused all this havoc with our identities."

"We find these bastards rollin' in cash what's the play?" Bugout inquired. "Because I'm out for blood."

P-Man rubbed his facial hair. "There's a way to deal with mufuckaz. Even kids, son. Identify 'em and I'll tell you the play."

Chapter Twenty-Six

Crip and Bloods Fight
Van Dolan Park
Mt. Vernon, NY

"I hate these punk ass Blood nyggas," Coldhearted heard a new Black student say as they sat in their 3rd period homeroom class. "Mufuckaz think they run shit."

"Who you talkin' to, Blood?" a boy named Oscar asked him.

The young man who had made the incendiary comment stood on his own. "I'm talkin' to anyone in range nygga, and ain't no bs this way, homie. C's all across the board. What up wit it, cuz?"

The new young man stood up throwing up them C's. The two students were sent to the principal's office but vowed to meet up after school to settle it like gangstas.

Coldhearted texted his crew. Some had graduated and were no longer at Mt. Vernon High School. This included Savage Hood Girlz. Coldhearted told them that there was going to be a fight at Van Dolan Park after school broke. Rock texted everyone back to come out flying *Savage Hoodz* jackets and colors so they'd be easy to recognize amongst all the crews and crowds that would be mobbin' through.

Coldhearted cut school early and had Liza pick him up around the side of the school. Her classes were over at 1:00 PM anyway so it was perfect timing. They headed straight home where they got dressed. Rock had given the entire team Savage Hoodz and Savage Hood Girlz leather jackets so that's what Coldhearted wore. He gave Liza a second one he had.

He put that black flag in one back pocket and the $100 bill bandana he tied around his head. He threw on the black New York Yankee fitted cap to top it off.

"Baby, go get my diamond chain," he told her.

She went to the drawer where he kept all off his chains, bracelets, rings and

watches. "You hardly wear your jewelry. Why now?"

"I'm still not," he said taking the expensive chain from her. "My mami is."

She lit up with a smile. "So, why these nyggas fightin' and why you and me getting dressed up for it?"

He put the 75-inch chain around her neck and pat frisked her like he was looking for a wire. "You a cop, a reporter or author?" he joked with her.

"Boy!" she retorted. "You just wanted to feel that ass."

"Uhn huhn," he admitted. "C'mon."

He stopped in the kitchen and pulled the refrigerator out. Behind it was a wall

safe he'd recently had installed. He opened it and removed two Walther PK .380's and put them into his inside jacket pockets.

They left and drove to the park with at least 45 minutes to spare but they could see that many of the Junior and Senior kids who were let out early, like Liza, were already there. Soon, Rock pulled up in the corner of the parking lot next to where Coldhearted sat on the passenger's side of the sleek new Cadillac Escalade.

Coldhearted leaned out the window, taking a real long look at the Dodge Viper SRT GT Coupe Rock pulled up in. Gunmetal pearl exterior with black sabelt, Nappa leather, Alcantara trim seats. 8.4- Liter V-10 SFI engine paired to a 6-speed manual transmission. Rock knew how to find the best and he didn't hesitate dropping the $140,000 on a collector to get it either.

"Damn that thing is nice!" Coldhearted said.

"I know, you like that?" Rock grinned, getting out of the beautiful ride. He was iced out, designer black jeans, the latest Jordans, black leather Savage Hoodz jacket, platinum ice grill and Rolex Submariner watch. "Now...."

Coldhearted rolled the window all the way down and looked at Rock.

"What yo lil ass up to nygga?" Rock asked. "What's up, Liza? Y'all look nice."

"Hey, Rock, thank you," she returned with a smile.

Coldhearted kept his eyes peeled. "A lot of Crips been comin' through Money Earnin' Mt. Vernon lately. This kid in my school is mobbed up with a buncha dem nyggas and the Bloods don't like it. So, there's been a lot of mouthin' goin on. Today these two nyggas set tripped and called it. So, here we are."

"So," Rock said as a whole line of Savage Hoodz and Savage Hood Girlz cars and motorcycles came roaring into the parking lot. "What's the play on our part?"

"I think Savage Hoodz and Crips should be allies," Coldhearted said as the rest of the crew encircled him and Rock. "Like that Crip nygga told that bitch ass Blood nygga these mufuckaz think they run shit."

"That's cuz they do," Chubb told him.

Rock, Dojo, Shadow, Choir Boy, Wolfman, Orca, Tommy Gunz, Hk, Mac-11, Sonja, Alejandra, Shay, Joyce, Blue Eyez, Diamond Girl, Bhad Barbie, Sunny, Ava Applez and Juicy P all nodded in agreement. The Blood presence was heavy in Mt. Vernon.

"What I'm saying is they don't *have to,*" Coldhearted stated. "If we put our money behind some of these nyggaz in the studio we can attract a thousand of em to come right here and help us shut these mufuckaz *down.*"

Tommy Gunz supported Coldhearted's view. "Yeah, son. They only bullies cuz the playing field ain't even. He ain't sayin let's jump in the fight cuz we know we can't do that."

A bunch of Blood nyggaz came through at the same time a convoy of cars filled

with Crip nyggaz entered and parked on the far side of the parking lot. Coldhearted recognized the young Crip cat who came ready to knuckle up. He had his shirt off and everyone could see that he was of average height, brown skin, with gang tatoos all over his chest and back. Coldhearted didn't know his name but he was a *"real"* Crip in his book. There were a lot of wannabee gangstas running around talking that life when they wasn't even about that life. That was Coldhearted's view of the majority of the Bloods at his school. Them nyggaz was watching Youtube clips of how "real" Blood nyggaz from Compton and South Central got down and they copycatted them. Coldhearted labelled them "Blood impostors."

But dude standing in the middle of the parking lot flexin' had a blue rag hanging out of his left back pocket. He was bare knuckled, ready to go.

The Blood cat he had called out arrived with his own mob of seven other Bloods. There had to be at least 40 to 50 Crips out there semi circled on one side of the parking lot and approximately 60 to 70 Bloods on the other side. All of the spectators kind of played the background.

Coldhearted and Liza walked over to where the Crips stood.

"Fuck this young nygga doin'?" Rock whispered.

Chubb started to walk over there but Rock stopped him. "Dont get too close. Them mufuckaz guaranteed to have guns."

"What set you from?" a 20-plus year old Black man with dreads asked Coldhearted.

Coldhearted turned around and showed him. "We Savage Hoodz. We witchu, nygga."

The Crip looked at him and back over at all the others in black leather jackets. He noticed all the top notch vehicles and bikes they had and knew the crew was rich.

"You ever heard of Savage Hoodz Records?" Coldhearted asked.

Several Crips standing by overheard the conversations and the seed was planted. Rock had been upgrading the SHZ Recording Studio and Coldhearted was pushing his agenda. The Hoodz couldn't stand the Bloods so why not use the Crips to eventually exterminate them? To do that, first they had to be befriended. And then empowered. And what Rock had going on they had the cashflow to do it with.

The fight began with the Crip, grips up throwing a soft jab at the Blood and missing. They both were about the same size. They were over-hyped to kill each other so they ran into each others wild punches and grabbed each other. They started wrestling. The Crip was able to lift the Blood up high and body slam him on his back super hard!

The Crip had him pinned at that point and rained down blow after blow to his head face, arms and body!

"This ain't no fun! The Crip jumped up off of dude. "Get up, foo!"

"Fuck nygga!" The Blood cat was back up with his lip busted and right eye twitching from getting hit. He rushed at the off, swinging a mighty right cross that caught the Crip and made him stumble backwards!

But the onrushing Blood came at him too fast and the Crip used that momentum to trip him up and throw him to the ground. This time he let him get up and saw that the Blood was losing stamina.

"Oh, you smoke, nygga!?" the Crip said, moving in with a barrage of body and one good face shot. "You a cigarette sucker?"

Then from down south came the uppercut that rocked him straight to sleep! The Crip stood there and let him drop, crashing to the asphalt!

"Yeah!" The young Crip threw up them C's just as a lone

cop car came rolling into the park! Everybody scrambled to their vehicles!

"C'mon, son, we gotchu!" Coldhearted tapped the Crip on his back and ran towards his parked caddy! The Crip and two of his homiez followed. "Go, mami! Follow Rock! Stay right on his ass!"

"They call you Coldhearted," the Crip said as Liza Peeled out. "You in my class."

"Yeah and this wifey, Liza," Coldhearted told the three young Crip cats.

"I'm Double Deuce," the Crip said in an unmistakable South Central, Los Angeles lingo. "Reppin' that Rollin Sixties Neighborhood Crip set. In the back is my cousins Double J and Spooky."

"All three of y'all Neighborhood?" Coldhearted inquired.

"Yeah," Deuce answered.

"Hold on!" Liza said making a hard right behind Rock who lost her once they peeled out of the mouth of the parking lot.

Coldhearted got a text that everyone was meeting at the Dairy Queen on North Avenue in New Rochelle. He decided not to follow them. Instead, he looked out the side view mirror to see that all was clear.

"What's Savage Hoodz, homie?" Deuce asked, seeing the jackets.

"That's *my* gang, son," Coldhearted informed them. "Hey, baby."

"Huhn?" Liza answered him.

"Y'all nyggaz hungry?" Coldhearted asked them.

"Hell yeah, but we ain't got no paper," Double J said: "Not really."

"Shid, I got ten," Spooky offered.

"Yeah, I got a dub," Deuce told Coldhearted. "Where y'all talkin' 'bout though?"

"Them nyggaz all went to Dairy Queen," he told his girl. "Wanna ditch 'em?"

Liza smiled and said, "No! You are so crazy. You made everybody come out, Daddy! Let's go."

"Aight. They in New Ro on North Avenue," he said, changing his mind. "Ayo, Deuce... we headin' out to Dairy Queen. My crew out there. Can any of y'all Crip nyggaz rap?"

"Hell yeah," Double J said and he just started spitting mad bars.

Coldhearted turned in his seat after putting a *Shook Ones*, by Mobb Deep, beat on the Escalade's sound system. Double J was a beast. He killed that *Shook Ones* beat.

Coldhearted stared at Liza.

"What?" she demanded as she drove. "You're up to something. What is it?"

He only smiled.

Chapter Twenty-Seven

La Cocina Restaurant
New Rochelle, NY

Rock almost asked the young thug the same exact thing. "What's really goin' on in that mind of yours, C?"

Coldheated sat back in his seat after having had enough of all the lobster and fried calamari at *La Cocina Restaurant* in New Rochelle. No one wanted Dairy Queen's hot dogs or hamburgers so they drove up the street to a new Dominican restaurant.

"You put all that money into that studio," Coldhearted reminded him in a low voice. The entire Savage Hoodz and

Savage Hood Girlz were at the restaurant. "When you gon' pull the trigger, Rock?"

Chubb overheard them talking. "I been working on my shit. Put me in the booth."

Coldhearted made a c'mon now, son, face. Half the SHZ nyggaz and bitches got bars. Double J got *talent*. And I need ten percent of each Crip nygga contract cuz it was my idea to bring them into our circle."

Rock stared at Coldhearted. "I know you, C. Imma sign Double J but don't use these niggas for your wild ass, personal agenda against the Pirus."

"Man, whateva," Coldhearted waved him off, not making any promises. "I'm just tryna make us stronger."

Rock used his strand to drink his Pepsi. "I get that and we need to do more to launder money. I had no real idea that we could pull in so much from this underworld store. None of us thought that. So, makin' the SHZ label pop again would be good because we got alot of fake records to make to launder this fuckin' cash we gettin'."

"So, put the APB out on all the Crips who tryna get they shit on wax," Chubb nearly whispered.

"Ten percent too much, too, nygga," Rock told Cold-hearted. "You trippin' we got a whole squad that need job titles, a check, etcetera. Share the love, C."

Coldhearted nodded.

"Double J!" Rock called him over to the booth next to

theirs where Double J was entertaining a couple of the SHZ Girlz. "Wanna come over here for a minute?"

Seconds later Double J was standing with his hands on the back of Coldhearted's chair, looking at Rock. "What's happenin' wit it, cuz?"

"Whattayu think about signin' a contract with Savage Hoodz Records?" Rock asked him. "SHZ started out as a hip hop crew and had some successes. But original members started getting' locked up, shot up, and the label went nowhere. But the name survived, and we're in a real good position to restart the label."

"Maaan, my moms will *trip*," Double J said. "Already bad enough I'm fuckin' up in school. What'll I have to do?"

"Stay in school for one," Rock told him. "I still need to get a producer and get our staff tight. But the money and everything else is there. You need to get in the studio. Ayo, Deuce..."

"What up?" Deuce sat by listening.

"You and Spooky rap?"

"Hell nah," Deuce answered. "Wish I did cuz I'm tryna get it. My cousin, J hot wit it though. We all was locked up in juvie out in L.A. All he did was write raps all day and battle nyggaz in the yard."

Double J nodded. "Me and Spooky is brothers. Our mom and Deuce mom moved

out here to keep California from makin' us a ward of the state. If we stayed we woulda been sent to CYA."

"C-Y-A?" Coldhearted asked.

"California Youth Authority," Deuce said.

All of the SHZ and SHZ Girlz were listening in now.

"So y'all be thuggin'," Tommy Gunz probed.

"Fuck yeah," Double J said.

Double J was the light skinned pretty boy of the three. He had nicely braided cornrows, tall, he had a deep voice and many of the SHZ Girlz liked his charm. Spooky was the complete opposite. He was dark skinned, 16 years old - a year older than Double J - and though not an attractive young man the women loved him because he was also tall, well-built and funnier than a mufucka.

"We chillin' though," Spooky told them. "Our moms begged us to graduate and stay away from them laws."

Deuce spoke up. "But nyggas is fake as shit. Ain't put in no real work and walkin' around wit' tattoo tears. I promote Crip fam recruitment but these East Coast nyggaz is claimin' a set they never even visited or paid homage to. If we bring you into Rollin 60's I *require* you to take that ass out there and meet the homiez outta respect."

"Like, we know Blood niggaz we get money wit out L.A.," Spooky added. "The big homiez that brought us up taught us that it's the *green* that means everything so get it wit' the Devil if you have to. I just can't stand these frontin ass Bloods up here in Mt. Vernon.

Coldhearted looked across the table at Orca and winked at him. "Us neither, homie."

"Anyhow," Rock said. "Y'all stay outta trouble, and stay in school. Lemme get wit my lawyer so we can create a general contract. And we'll meet with you and your moms. As for Deuce and Spooky y'all want jobs wit SHZ?"

"Jobs? Paycheck jobs?" Spooky asked.

"Yeah you want a paycheck?" Rock inquired.

Double J answered that. "I'm tellin' you, our mothers be on our top about everything. If we come home wit' cash, they'll think we stole it or sold dope to get it."

"What will the jobs be?" Deuce asked.

"Talent scouts," Rock offered. "Right now, we wanna focus on all Crips. You know any bonafide G nyggaz wit' dope material?"

Duece nodded. "My whole fucking crew back home in L.A. The Hover Dover Blood Removers."

"Y'all job is to get 'em in the studio," Rock told him. "Chubb, give these boys a lil taste."

Chubb pulled out a thick wad of $100 bills and handed several of them to each young Crip.

Rock pointed to Coldhearted. "He's y'all's boss. Everything will be coordinated through him. He's Chief Recruiter."

"We get a signin' bonus for the contract?" Double J inquired.

Rock thought that over. "You got enough for a whole album or mixtape?"

Double J scoffed. "I got mad rhymes."

Rock nodded. "I don't see why not. Lemme throw

together some managers, promoters, a producer, engineer and we'll make it happen. Just so you know, we ain't been in the game in a long time. We just getting' started. But we been getting' money from the streets among other places... so..."

"Shiiid, that's not hard to tell," Spooky said. "Yo whole mob got Benzes, BMW's,

Coldhearted got the Lac truck, and you have some ole James Bond shit."

Rock grinned. "That's a $140,000 Dodge Viper."

"Hundred forty *gees*?" Deuce's mouth dropped.

"SHZ Records is strong and ready to sign new artists," Rock said. "Youse tell ya Crip homiez that the Blue is just who we choose to align ourselves with at this time."

"Aight, we gotta get home." Deuce and his cousins stood up. "Glad we ran into each other in the same class, C."

"I'll take you home," Coldhearted said.

Liza drove them back out to Mt. Vernon.

When they arrived at an apartment building on South Elm Street Liza stopped.

"Ayo, C," Deuce spoke from the rear seats of the luxury Caddy.

"Yeah," Coldhearted responded.

"So, we ain't movin' no coke, no dope, nothin'?" Deuce asked. "I mean straight up."

"Why you ask that?"

Double J replied to that. "We just ain't met no one like

y'all. Aside from the cash, cars, clothes and jewelry look at y'all women. They class A."

Coldhearted nodded. "Y'all ain't selling no dope. I mean what you see is what you see. I'll talk to you at school. Gotta get my two babies to sleep."

"Okay," Deuce hesitated. "You mean... oh, Liza. Ya wifey pregnant! You gonna have a kid, man?!"

Coldhearted nodded.

"That's wassup!" Deuce said.

They all called it a night.

Chapter Twenty-Eight

Westchester County Mall

Saturday 1:oo PM

"**H**ey sweet thing," Rock called out to the bombshell light skinned babe with the almond-shaped light gray eyes. She was tall for a female, 5 feet 1o inches perhaps, had a body to die for and she was some sort of exotic mixture. "May I stop you for just a second?"

"Huhn?"

"Dann," Rock said. "Your voice even pretty."

She smiled. "Thank you," she said.

Rock was in the parking lot of the Westchester County

Mall with the entire Savage Hoodz squad. It looked like a car show out there. Rock, of course, brought out the Viper. But even more than that Savage Hoodz Records was recording a video for Double J's hit record: *"I'm High."*

A company from out of Stamford, Connecticut – Holman Luxury Motorcars - was hired to bring down some of its most opulent vehicles for the 2-day shoot. Each member of SHZ had their own assigned luxury car and Westchester County Mall owners had closed of the entire east end side of their parking lot for a sizeable SHZ check the only spectators that were allowed were only the best looking females that had answered the radio call at several of NYC's most popular radio stations.

Rock seen this supermodel type with the Chinese eyes and his heart skipped a beat.

"I'm Rock," he introduced himself by giving her a business card and a Savage Hoodz T-shirt.

"Rock!" Diamond Girl chided him. "That's a girl! You givin' her that big ass T-shirt."

Rock looked at the T-shirt and held it up to the beauty that was making him lose his senses. "Yeah ... this shit's like 5X."

"Least you making her laugh," Diamond Girl said, looking at the Amazon with the dazzling eyes. "Here, girl. Here's a Pink Savage Hood Girlz Tee and tank top, and a nice lil baseball hat to go wit it."

"I can sleep in his big T-shirt," the girl said.

"See, Diamond Girl? She likes my big T," Rock smiled.

Diamond Girl was a thick, 5 feet 5 inch, 160 pound, white girl with natural brownish-red hair. She had curves like a country road, pretty pink lip's and the girl knew how to dress.

"Oh, so you behind all this?" the babe asked, looking at the business card. "CEO of Savage Hoodz Records."

He nodded. "You don't have a demo do you?"

"God no," She laughed. "Just came to see the video shot. I love that *I'm High* record. It's like I smoke I'm proud, I'm happy and fuck you if you don't like it."

"Excuse me if I'm out of pocket," Rock said to her. "But you look good. You have a pretty voice. A sexy laugh. You smell mad good. You smoke. You cuss. And you the most exotic woman I ever seen. Please. PLEASE tell me-"

"I'm single," she laughed. "You are so funny. And you look good, too."

He put his hands together, closed his eyes, and mouthed a small prayer of "*Thank you God,*" to heaven which made her laugh even more.

"What do you like to eat, where would you like to go, etcetera, etcetera," he asked.

She shrugged. "Surprise me."

"What's your number?" he asked, handing her his cellphone. "Put it in there with your name."

"Okay... you got a million girls out here..." she let that hang in the air.

"Baby and it would take a million of them to compare to one of you," Rock told her. "As a matter of fact how bout you appear in this video?"

She was surprised. "Really?"

"Put your stuff in here," he said, indicating his Dodge Viper sitting nearby. "They 'bout ready to film, Tay... Taizhan?"

"*Taizhan*," she smiled. "*Tie* like necktie and the Z and the H together sorta like a J and H together. *Taizhan*."

"Taizhan," Rock said, letting her drop her things into the front seat of the Viper. "Now you get into the driver's seat."

He showed her how to adjust the seat to her liking. "Your window will be down and you'll just follow the other cars in a figure eight."

"Fast?" she inquired.

"No, no, no," he said. "The opposite. This way everybody will see that lovely face."

"How do you -" she asked, looking for the ignition.

"Start it up?" He said. She nodded and he learned in across her and pushed a button. The engine came to life and so and their private parts. She smiled shyly and smelled his closeness to her. He felt the same current of electricity exchange between them as he pushed his way back outside of the car. "You like how that engine vibrates? Kinda like a lion's roar at first ... and then he settles down, huhn?"

"Mm hm," she nodded. "This is nice."

He closed the door and spoke to her. "All of my peoples

are out here today makin' a paycheck for about fourteen hundred for two days work. You want the job?"

Taizhan nodded. "I'm down with whatever you wanna do with me," she flirted.

He stepped back and shook his head. "Giirrrill…"

Whoever she was she damn sure knew how to knock a nygga senseless, he thought, as the shooting of the video began.

Chapter Twenty-Nine

Bugout was inside of their have gym working out when Taizhan entered their Croton On The Hudson luxury apartment. He finished running the daily five miles on the Peleton and removed his earbuds. He was drenched in perspiration as he guzzled the entire quart of Gatorade.

He heard the shower running as he walked back towards the master bedroom. Before he got there he took off his shorts and underwear. He entered and noticed that Taizhan had been on a shopping spree. There were bags from Louis Vuitton, Burberry, Birkin, Tiffany & Co. and more, sitting alongside the bed on the floor.

She had taken off her panties and bra set along with the peach Prada dress that was pooled on the floor. He picked up the panties and noticed that they were saturated with her secretions. He carried them into the bathroom where she was humming a Mary J. Blige song and using a large pink cloth to soap up and scrub her magnificent body with.

He opened up the shower door and gazed at her while he brought the panties up to his face, closed his eyes and inhaled her musky scent. She noticed how strong and powerful his erection was. It reminded her of a long, thick plantain with mad veins pulsating all over it. She observed how he had perspiration dripping down his muscular 5 foot 11 inch body.

She watched his face closely, though, because she both loved and feared Bugout. He was a ruthless, murderous man. And, just as she thought the thought, he snatched her by her long ponytail and slapped her so hard she tasted blood on the inside of her cheek where she'd bitten herself.

"Open your eyes!" he commanded her.

"Okay!" she cried, surprised by the stinging slap.

He looked at her. Out of fear she grabbed the body wash and squirted liberal amounts all over his chest, stomach, privates, and everywhere else. She bathed him as if he were a Hebrew god and she was nothing more than a pretty slave. She bathed and massaged him.

When they were both fully rinsed off he grabbed her by

her arm and pulled her into the bedroom. "Tell me why your pussy was so wet? Why your panties so soggy?" he demanded.

She was afraid to speak.

He slapped her again. She fell onto the bed and she scooted up with her yellow thighs wide open. He could see the light reflect off of the slightly open pink mucous membrane lining of her inner passage. Her clitoris was even poking out of the fleshy hood that covered it. It was erect, excited.

"You fucked that nygga didn't you?" Bugout asked her. "You been gone two days... did you fuck him?"

Taizhan nodded slowly as she stuck her middle finger in between her swollen labia and bathed it in her juices. He moved up onto the bed and lay beside her while she stroked her clit.

"I can tell how your flower opens that you was fucked," he said. "Start from the beginning... tell me everything."

"He took me to *Le Francia* - a fancy French restaurant where we had a corner booth," she started as she lay between his legs and kissed his mushroom-shaped cockhead. She licked it all around as she spoke. "He couldn't keep his hands off of me. I kept flirting with him and we kissed like tomorrow would never come. He could see my, nipples poking out against the thin material of my Prada dress and he pulled on them and teased them."

She used her delicate hands to caress his big balls and

tongue his throbbing dick until it looked like it would explode like a stick of dynamite. She took him down to her pretty mouth and gave him super sloppy head for a minute. Her fingers made their way down, to her pussy as she deep throated him. She got off on this freaky shit, too.

"What else he do?" Bugout inquired.

"Before we even ate he was fingering my pussy, makin' me so wet," she whispered in a voice that quivered while she pinched her hot clit. "He fed me and I fed him. He put my hand on his huge dick and I filled it out. Our booth was private so I went down on him right there."

"Was he bigger, smaller, wider than me?"

"Mmm," she sucked him in and out of her mouth and throat at breakneck speed. "Bigger, Daddy. He had the biggest fuckin black dick..."

She had his toes curling. She spit on his dick and worked it in and out of her mouth like crazy. "He had so much pre-cum, Daddy. He tasted so delicious slidin' in and out of my mouth and throat. I couldn't fit it all in but he grabbed my head and forced his monster into my throat. He made me take it all."

"Right at the table?"

"Yeah but I wouldn't let him cum." She went back to slurping Bugout's member in and out of her wet mouth. "He took me to his house and we were out of our clothes in under a minute. He threw me on the bed and ate my pussy sooo good. He kissed my clit... blew on it... rubbed his face all into me, enjoying my smell and taste. He flipped me over and ate my ass while finger fucking me with three large fingers."

"Did he fuck you?"

"Oh god, yes!" she excitedly whimpered as she got on top of him. "Like this first. He wanted me on top... he said he wanted to watch my pointy nipples and suck on them. He left marks. See?"

Bugout did see the bite marks Rock had left on her upturned breasts. She was so horny and ready to be fucked. She rode up and down on top of him like a rodeo champ. She broke out in a dripping sweat.

"He made me ride his big dick like this," she panted and swiveled her hips left and right and in a circular motion. She fell forward and Bugout grabbed her ass and bit her nipples. "I could feel him inside of my navel! Fuck! Oooouuu, fuck me, Daddy!"

Bugout couldn't take anymore. He flipped her over missionary and fucked her all the way until he blasted cum all up inside of her she screamed her own orgasm into his ear, biting him and scratching his back.

Minutes passed before either of them said anything.

"You find anything to point that them nyggas hacked us?" Bugout asked her.

She was careful how she answered. "Too early to tell. It was only two days."

Bugout turned to her and hit her so hard that she nearly blacked out. She hit the floor and he was on top of her, slapping her in the face over and over. She covered herself with her arms and he punched her several times.

"Bitch!" he barked at her. "If you tryna bullshit me think again! Don't catch feelings for that chump or I'll kill you too! Don't try to fuckin' play me I'll kill you and him! You hear me?!"

Taizhan was crying. "Yes! Yes! Please don't hurt me!" she begged.

Sometimes she didn't get Bugout. She did everything to prove her loyalty and he still punished her. Sometimes he was even more severe. As Bugout lay asleep that night next to her she wished she could return to her mother, a doctor, and her father a dentist, but she had chosen the fast life with an abusive alcoholic, sexually depraved, gangster. She was his submissive slave.

A something in front of others.

A nothing at all times in between.

Coldhearted & Liza's

Mt. Vernon, NY

Wednesday 7:30 PM

Chapter Thirty

Coldhearted, Chubb, Dojo, Shadow, Choir Boy, Wolfman, Orca, Tommy Gunz, HK, Mac-11, Sonja, Alejandra, Shay, Joyce, Blue Eyes, Diamond Girl, Bhad Barbie, Sunny, Ava Applez and Juicy P all walked into the house through the garage door entrance. That entranceway led directly into the laundry room of Coldhearted's house.

"Ayo, it's a bathroom there," Coldhearted pointed. "A laundry room sink there. The kitchen sink to the right. Sinks everywhere. Let's all wash our hands cuz my girl is sensitive about that and nobody wears shoes in house. So kick'em off in the laundry room."

"Papi that you?" Liza yelled.

"Yeah, I got company, mami!" he yelled back.

He walked into the kitchen and saw soul food being cooked as he washed his hands. He led his crew into the living room where he ran into Elizabeth and Lupé.

"Oh, Miss Lupé, Elizabeth." He was surprised to see them but he bounced back. He pointed at his crew. "These are my comrades. Comrades, Miss Lupé and wifey's mom, Elizabeth."

"How're youse?" Lupe greeted everyone. She was Daphne and Maria's mother. Elizabeth was Lupé's youngest sister.

Coldhearted exited while they each got acquainted. He ran into Liza in the hallway and kissed her. "What are they doin'?"

Liza, wearing a cute pink sweatsuit by Dior pointed at her protruding belly. "I'm havin' the baby with midwives and both my mom and her sister are midwives. Who better to help me through towards the end than family."

"Aight," he said. "I just hope they don't trip cuz of how I handled that shit wit' Papo-"

"Shh!" Liza quieted him, hugging him. "That's old," she assured him. "Trust ya, mami."

"I got the whole SHZ here," he told her.

"What? Why you ain't say nothing!?" She punched his arm.

"I just did."

"No, dummy, I mean like yesterday," she stated. "At least we coulda made more food."

"Don't worry," he assured her. "We'll order."

"Nonsense." She walked with him to the kitchen. She added another huge pot of boiling water to prepare rice and beans. She pulled several packages of steaks out of the deep freezer and thawed them under cold water in the kitchen sink.

Coldhearted came up from behind her and produced a diamond necklace which he put on her, kissing her neck from behind. She shrieked with delight and embraced him.

"Thank you, Papi!" she said sweetly. "Where all y'all comin' from?"

"The shootin' range and the studio," he told her.

"Shootin' range?" she frowned. "Where?"

"You know that the SHZ Hangout has a basement garage?" he asked her.

"I thought I heard someone say it was a horror scene down there," she mentioned.

He nodded. "They had it cleaned and made into a shootin' range."

"Mm smells goods," Elizabeth said as she came into the kitchen. "Hey, Sage, can I have a minute?"

He got up and stepped out into the laundry room with the chubby, but pretty, Latina woman.

"I don't have no beef with you," she said, extending her hand. He took it. "I don't agree with how you did Maria but I understand cuz you felt threatened."

"I don't have a beef with you either," he reciprocated. "Nor Maria and Papo. If they need money I'll help any of y'all."

"Me and Lupé are midwives and that's my daughter," Elizabeth asserted. "No one's gonna care for her like us. No one is better suited to see to her and the baby's safety. Is it okay?"

"I'm with that," he assured her.

Elizabeth took a deep breath. "I'm not tryna tell you what to do but we need a one hundred percent safe environment here. No drugs, no crime, no -"

He cut her short. "This is our sanctuary. I promise you."

Elizabeth was relieved on one hand but on the other hand Coldhearted made her nervous. In fact, he made her entire family afraid of him. History justified it. They could overlook the fact that Liza and he were cousins by adoption because there was no blood connection.

Sensing this he took Elizabeth and Lupé back to his and Liza's bedroom. He was a boy by age but he'd lost a boy's innocence a lifetime ago. In its place there was a boy who thought and carried himself like a man.

"Look," he said to Elizabeth.

From out of nowhere he hugged her which was startling to her but she hugged him back. He kissed her cheek. She nodded.

"I'm sorry about everything," he expressed to her as Liza came in. "Liza needs you. Our baby needs it's *Abuela*. So, no smoke. We all good, okay?"

Elizabeth nodded as Coldhearted also embraced Lupé. She was a petite woman who was darker than half of her family due to their half Dominican half Puerto Rican heritage. She looked like a native Indian in a lot of respects.

"We all good," Elizabeth replied to him.

"Hmph," Lupe said. "Why all the sudden change?"

He looked over at Liza. "She's why."

That made Elizabeth and Lupe melt.

"She's everything," he continued. "I love each strand of her hair. She's beautiful. I'll do anything for her."

"Es *mi hija*," Elizabeth smiled proudly.

"Let's eat you guys!" Liza urged them. "All this mushy mushy."

"Shut up, *hija*," Elizabeth said as they exited the bedroom.

Coldhearted went into the living room to holler at all the others. "Baby girl laced dinner for everybody. C'mon, Tommy, you can't fuck wit that XBOX anyway."

"Yeah right!" Tommy said pausing the game. There was money on the marble coffee table. "Don't nobody fuck wit' my game. I'm 'bout to take Orca's car payment money."

"Crazy as a mufucka nygga," Orca countered. "I'm already up two games on that ass."

They had a great get together that night. Coldhearted felt real good that Liza's mom was back on deck- That would go a long way with their baby about to arrive.

The Baby Is Born
Coldhearted Liza's
Mt. Vernon, NY

Chapter Thirty-One

The Baby Is Born
Coldhearted Liza's
Mt. Vernon, NY

Liza went into labor right after Coldhearted's 15th birthday. Fortunately, Elizabeth and Lupe were both not only her family but professionals. It was early in the day, just before he was about to go to school, when she woke up with severe pain in her back.

"Fuck!" she whined. "The baby!"

He went and woke up Lupe and Elizabeth. They examined Liza and knew right away that she was ready. They had already set up the living room for an underwater birth. Coldhearted pulled the children's pool from the garage and filled it with hot water as planned.

They had leased several pieces of expensive medical equipment that were set up in there also. It looked like a very comfortable hospital set up with the pool in the center, a heart and respiratory monitor, clean white towels, a weight scale and everything else they may need.

"Hey, C." Lupé called him over after she checked the water. "Get about a half bag

of ice and throw in here. It's too hot, baby."

He retrieved the ice and they cooled the water down enough for the baby's arrival. Coldhearted stood by as Lupé and Elizabeth put Liza down into the water. Coldhearted sent out a group text to SHZ: *"Baby on the way!"*

The baby was stubborn and kept Liza in labor for hours. By that time all of the SHZ Girlz were there. Then the boys arrived along with Rock, Chubb and their Mother Tanya. Coldhearted made all of them stay in the family room to give Liza privacy.

"This shit crazy I never been to no shit like this," Tommy Gunz said to everyone.

"Ayo, C!" Diamond Girl called out to him.

He popped into the family room. "Wassup?"

"Man, we all family here, let us see the underwater birth!" she pleaded. "We ain't never seen nothing like it. Please?"

"Yeah," Barbie said. "C'mon man."

"Lemme ask Liza," he relented. He went back to his girl and made the request.

"I don't give a fuck!" She screamed.

Lupé put a black T-shirt on Liza who was submerged in the pool from the breasts down. Elizabeth was in there with her, massaging her belly, urging her to push because the baby was coming. All of SHZ members entered and watched the beautiful Latina thrash and splash the water with her hands as she cried out in pain and agony.

"Here, it is - push, *mija!*" her mother urged her. "The head is right here!"

Liza pushed harder. The water turned a cloudy crimson and a turd floated on top, which was natural. Coldhearted removed it with a plastic bag which he tossed in a trashcan sitting nearby. He squeezed Liza's hand and she squeezed his harder.

"Here we are!" Elizabeth announced, pulling the baby all the way out of Liza. "You got a daughter, Sage! It's a girl!"

Lupé pinched the baby's pale cheeks as Elizabeth placed her on Liza's chest. The two midwives fussed around the baby, spanking her little butt until she started to cry louder.

"That's right, mamita," Lupe kissed the tiny infant. "We just want you to breathe. We're sorry."

Elizabeth looked at Coldhearted. "Not so Coldhearted right now, huhn, *mijo?* Seein' this?"

For the moment he was Sage Michael Thomas. An overwhelmed 15 year old boy whose 17 year old girlfriend had just given birth to his daughter. He didn't know it but tears were flowing down his face like raindrops on a windshield. He was shown how to cut the umbilical cord.

Seeing Coldhearted cry made all the SHZ Girls cry. Even some of the Hoodz had wet eyes. Nearly all of them had their phones out recording it. Then, to give Liza privacy, they all left the room. Everyone helped with the clean up.

Coldhearted literally carried Liza to the master bedroom and put her to bed. Lupé and Elizabeth had to chase him out so they could examine her vagina for ruptures. She only needed ten stitches. And then they had to get the baby to suckle on her breasts for the milk she'd need.

"Ayo," Rock said after the clean-up was over. He looked at his watch. "I haveta meet with some producers, Taizhan and a few other things. As soon as the baby has a name lemme know."

Coldhearted walked him to the door. "Double J records sellin'?"

Rock shook his head no. "But it's a numbers game. We spend a 100K and make it look like we legitimately made back 350k, 400k, we're winning. Legalizin' that dark net intake is expensive but we gotta look legit. Taxes need to be paid. If not we'll all get indicted. And I don't trust every SHZ mufucka to keep his or her mouth shut when them feds come knockin'."

Coldhearted liked Rock. "Me neither."

They handshake hugged and Rock exited.

"So, what's her name, homie?" Chubb asked as Coldhearted checked on his crew.

"C'mon, let's see if she done, feedin'," he told the group. "We been goin' back and forth on names…"

He walked back to his room and peeked in at Liza. "Mami?" he said.

"Hm?" she said tiredly.

"They wanna know what we named her."

"Tell 'em, Papi. Isabel, right?"

"Isabel," he told them.

"Aww," the girls said.

"What a beautiful name," Diamond Girl said as they all exited and said their goodbyes to Coldhearted.

Chapter Thirty-Two

Coldhearted was streamlining in single rap artists, rap duos, rap groups of three, four, and five, and even a rap supergroup that consisted of ten rap vocalists and a singer. He was regularly introducing some of the best West Coast's underground hip hop artists to Rock's producers and getting them into the studio.

They all had one thing in common. They were all Crips. Rock liked some of the talent among the 100 – plus artists they had tested so far but no one was of that superstar quality yet. SHZ Records was situated inside that an old building on Richlee Boulevard, Mt. Vernon.

The entire basement level was all studio space, and two offices Upstairs was a

failing bar that Rock eventually bought out with Tommy Gunz and Coldhearted in as silent partners. Rock had the bar renovated and renamed it *Garters* - a strip club.

On the same night that garters opened Coldhearted met up with Deuce and a smokey black nygga named OG Bobby Tate. He was about 5'7" with bulging rock hard muscles everywhere on his body. Bobby Tate was one of Deuce's uncles from Los Angeles who had migrated over with some of the other rappers Deuce had recruited. Bobby Tate couldn't rap to save his life. However, Coldhearted and Deuce had an understanding...

"That rap shit is cover for what we really out to do," Coldhearted had told Deuce months prior. *"Fuck rap, son. Tell the mufuckaz youse closest to if they tryna come out here we got another plan cooking in case the rap don't work out."*

Coldhearted liked Tate and Tate liked Coldhearted but Tate was ready to say fuck New York and head back to L.A. That is until Coldhearted stopped him.

"You thirty years old wit' no job, no education, prison half ya life," Coldhearted told him earlier.

"Ain't shit out here for me nygga," Tate had retorted.

"I'm pulling up on y'all tonight," Coldhearted had told Deuce and Tate. "Just you two."

Coldhearted picked them up at a Mcdonald's parking lot as planned. He drove them to an apartment building on Farnum Road. There were several other identical buildings in the small complex. Each one was only four stories high. They followed Coldhearted inside and they took the elevator upstairs.

Aside from a security lock there were three more locks on the door which Coldhearted used the keys to let them in. There was a doorbell camera and alarm that he had to disable as they went in which he did with his cellphone.

He locked all of the locks behind them and walked straight back to the master bedroom. Tate looked around, waiting. The apartment was nicely furnished. Everything was new. The bed was a beautiful Queen-size, immaculately made like it belonged in a showroom.

Tate lit up a cigarette and watched Coldhearted. He used two more keys to open up the closet. He pulled open the door and stepped inside. A moment later he came back out pointing a HK- 91 fully automatic machine gun at Tate at Deuce.

Tate stepped back. "Stop fuckin' around, mufucka."

"You play too much, nygga," Deuce told Coldheated with a sly grin on his face. "Lemme see that shit!"

Coldhearted gave the black foreboding weapon to his friend. "Go on in there."

OG Bobby Tate walked into the closet and paused as he looked at the three walls. "This somethin' out the movies my nygga. AK, Mac-11, AR-15, HK- 91, M-16, Glocks, Nines, Berettas, 380's ... what the fuck, C?"

"Look..." Coldhearted moved past him and opened up a steel safe in the rear of the closet.

Tate squatted down and whistled. "How the hell you get your hands on four kilos of coke, and – what's this?"

"Xstasy pills," Coldhearted informed him. "And two kilos of meth."

Coldhearted had a loaded PK 380 in his waist that neither of them knew about. He turned his back and walked towards the dresser. "Go 'head lock it all back up."

They did as he asked.

A small test of trust passed. So far at least.

"Aight, den, homie," Tate shrugged. "You got my attention."

Coldhearted nodded and sat on the sofa near the windows. "I love my crew but my crew is *soft!*"

Deuce laughed like: "Tell me about it."

"Don't get me wrong," Coldhearted said. "They come from awesome middle, upper middle class peoples and they pass every test at school, that type thing. They gifted hackers led by the right kinda suburb thug nygga."

"Rock," Tate guessed.

"Tommy Gunz, too," Coldhearted added. "But Rock had the family and the connects handed down to him to do what he do. He put together this underworld superstore - sorta like a mini Amazon - where guns, drugs and other illegal shit can be bought on the dark net. VULKANIKA-CYD.onion."

"You don't like it?" Tate asked.

Coldhearted shook his head. "I love it but only because I know how to fuck wit the dark net. Do *you*?"

Tate shook his head no.

"*Exactly*." Coldhearted cleared his throat. "My thing is there's droves of nyggas that don't know shit 'bout the software they need to buy to even start that walk into the dark net. I only know cuz I was moved here and made friends wit them. I'm a hood nygga. A Brooklyn nigga. These cats up here are bein' *bullied*, robbed, *took* ... by nyggas who get it from the streets. My crew, I admit, is getting' rich off that dark net shit but they talent may be the computer, mine is intelligence."

"How old are you if you don't mind?" Tate asked.

"Sixteen soon," he revealed.

"Damn," Tate muttered. "I swore you was older."

"Anyway," Coldhearted went on. "My intellect says to leave that computer shit alone cuz the feds will come to smash up the whole machine. So, I see a goldmine in the streets but the Blood nyggaz got mufuckaz scared to come out and get it. Between here and upper Bronx it's Blood *infested*."

Tate understood. "I see. So, you want to mount a takeover."

"A *Crip Gang* takeover," Coldhearted put it into perspective. "They just the right ones needed for it."

"And you think that why?" Tate asked, scoffing. "Cuz of some drugs and guns you got - some *money?*"

"Are you talkin' *down* to me?"

The mood suddenly shifted in the room. Tate shrugged. "I ain't bein disrespectful. I'm just bein' how other nyggaz I know will be when we line 'em up here. You show off guns, money, and drugs... nyggas will follow you for awhile. But only cuz they wanna kill you for ya shit. Or kidnap someone you love for ransom and kill them for the hatred they have for you once you pay. Cuz who are you? What work *you* put in?"

Coldhearted thought back to when Liza made him delete the machete killing video. At least she thought the video was deleted. He chuckled to himself.

"What's funny?" Tate asked him while Deuce stood idly by.

"You, nygga," Coldhearted said slowly. "I wish any nygga would try to take *anything* of mines. Or kidnap *anybody* of mines."

OG Tate stared at him.

"That whatchu thinkin'?" Coldhearted stood up, ready to blow holes in Tate and Deuce.

"You missed my point," Tate said quickly. "Calm down, man."

Coldhearted pulled out his phone and accessed the dark net. "Fuck ya point. Don't even think that shit cuz I'll kill you just for thinkin' it over my daughter."

Tate looked at Deuce like: *"is this nygga crazy?"*

Coldhearted gave the phone to Tate.

"That's a Blood nygga," he explained.

Tate turned the volume up on the phone and was transfixed by what he saw. Coldhearted cut D-Slice's balls open. And, later in the video, he decapitated him.

"Oh, shit!!" Tate and Deuce exclaimed loudly together.

Tate stared at the sheer brutality of what Coldhearted did with that blade and raised his eyebrows up. "Damn, homie..."

"Now if I fuck witchu and your nyggas *really* knew me," Coldhearted stated, "They prolly wouldn't even wanna fuck wit' me."

Tate gave him the phone back. "Nah, that ain't true. Nyggas follow nyggas they fear, love and respect."

Coldhearted sat back on the sofa.

Deuce and Tate sat on the side of the bed.

Tate spoke up. "Aight. You were talking about a takeover..."

Chapter Thirty-Three

Farnum Road Stashouse
Mt. Vernon, NY

Coldhearted took off the sweatshirt he was wearing and reached behind his neck. He slowly withdrew "Heartless" from the sheath he kept strapped to his back. OG Bobby Tate also saw the pistol in his waist.

"Youse a coldblooded gangster youngin', huh?" Tate asked with an admirable smile. "I see why they call you Coldhearted."

"Yeah," was all he said back.

"So, lay this shit out, C," Tate said in an open-handed gesture as he spoke.

Coldhearted sparked up a blunt and passed it to Tate. "Savage Hoodz got the studio thing poppin' off and then there's proceeds from VULKANIKACYD. What we have is the dope, coke, the artillery and we ran even cover this new craze of K2, molly, and prescription pain pills like Oxycontin."

"The shit we *don't* have?" Tate wisely asked.

Coldhearted nodded. "Best question on the table, son. Cuz this where I don't have it planned. You the O.G... We high school cats. What's your take?"

OG Bobby Tate saw the holes in the plan and he immediately understood that Coldhearted was choosing him to plug up such holes. But what Tate wanted to fully understand was what exactly was his role going to be and what was in it for him.

"Yo, cuzz, lemme tell you," Tate started. "I can help you put this shit together. But not all of the nyggas and nyggettes I bring out here I'm gonna know personally. You need to be hands off-"

Coldhearted held his hand up, stopping him. "Except when a mufucka needs his or her head chopped off. We can't be out here littering the street wit bodies either - if we can help it.

"Every now and then we gon have to," Tate told him. "Especially in the beginning. But if you wanna be assassin that's cool. But what you really need is layers and layers of protection. Meanin' you have other nyggas in frontline positions while you call the real shots in the background. At least to an extent."

Tate paused to recapture his earlier thoughts before Coldhearted interrupted him. "You want a big Crip Army out here. Full of Blood Removers. My nephew can't stand the Bloods and neither can you. Lemme school both of y'all young nyggas. My nephew and I are both Rollin 60s Neighborhood Crips and not all Crips will raise up against Bloods. And since I been out here Deuce and his potnas been invitin' over other Neighborhood Crips that *ain't* Rollin 60s. Not that that's a bad thing but I know certain Neighborhood Crips that go against each other."

"I thought y'all all stuck together," Coldhearted said.

OG Bobby Tate disagreed. "Maaan, look. L. A. is worser than New York and Chicago. There's at least a hundred Crip gangs in L.A. The youngstas don't pay attention to that cuz they eyes is just on they own gang. In L.A. it's all divided, so as people we're divided. Mid City, West L.A., San Pedro, we all over out there. The hoods are crazy. West Adams, Jefferson Park, Leimert Park, Hyde Park, Crenshaw, University Park, you got South L.A., Eastside, Venice, Watts-"

"West Athens," Deuce injected.

Tate pointed at Deuce. "West Athens, Compton, Lynwood and more. Aight, the way you importing Crips in to Savage Hoodz Records and all is cool but I don't know if that shit'll work longterm. And if you have us bring over some killaz to set it off on the Black P. Stones the bodies is gonna pile up on the street."

"And that's what I don't want," Coldhearted said. "I'm thinking more like puttin' them mufuckaz in the trunk and makin' 'em disappear."

Tate thought about it. "It *sounds* good. But you said it's Blood *infested* out here and northern Bronx."

Coldhearted nodded. "Five fifties everywhere."

"Listen to me, C, okay?" Tate sat forward. "If you want a army to come in and take out a handful of these cats we can do that. But it's infested and infestations take discipline, calculation and time. It has to happen organically. Now the guns, the work - all that is good. But what'll happen when you get a hundred, two hundred, etcetera, at SHZ who got a dream but the record deal ain't payin' bills?" "Return to L. A.?" Coldhearted saw his point.

Tate slowly nodded. "Exactly."

"Nyggaz need cribs, jobs, cars," Deuce rattled off a few examples.

"A hustle," Tate told him. "Coldhearted has the hustle part covered. It's a fuckin' goldmine out here. That's why them Black P Stones is protectin' this shit like it's their own turf. We haveta be careful cuz they willin' to kill and die for it, too, obviously."

Coldhearted said it all more clearly now. "So, Tate, you my OG - you the Capo of all this shit. The first thing I'ma tell you is that I co-own *Garters* wit Rock and Tommy Gunz. We gonna have that whole area jumpin' wit deals inside them apartments we gonna rent around there. You just gotta get them strippers to set up trustworthy contacts. Put enforcers in place to protect everything."

OG Bobby Tate nodded. "Now you talkin'. That's a good start. How many apartments for rent over in that area?"

"Dozens," Coldhearted told him. "We need to cop as many of those units as we can without them bein' connected to us. Can you do it, OG?"

Tate nodded. "You made me Capo so trust me to be Capo. You ain't dealin' wit no clown. I'll have a L.A. babe set up a L.L.C. here in New York as a construction company and rent the units through the company's bank accounts. And we can use the units to do deals in, hide in..."

"Live in, stash shit in, whatever," Coldhearted said with a shrug. "And since we getting' the *Garters* girls involved we need one particular spot set up for VULKANIKACYD to keep Rock and Tommy happy. They can have that shit cuz the feds comin' for it. I don't know when but they comin'. That's why I'm headin' to the streets for mines. That's how we gonna get it."

Tate had a sense of pride in dealing with Coldhearted. At first, the South Central Los Angeles O.G. gangster wasn't feeling him at all but as they spent more time talking and planning Tate was growing increasingly confident in the youngster's vision.

"I gotta get outta here," Coldhearted said as he sent Liza a text. "I have other stashouses like this one. I brought you here to show you a sample of what I been cookin up."

He made sure everything was locked up and after they left he called Liza. Tate and Deuce sat inside of his Cadillac SUV while he was on the phone.

"That nygga already rich ain't he?" Tate asked his nephew. "He gotta be papered up, huhn?"

"Hell yeah, look," Deuce said, showing his uncle the online video where Kato had beheaded a man, the woman, and lunged at the cops with a bloody machete in one hand and five year old Sage Michael Thomas in his other.

Tate was transfixed. He took his nephew's cellphone and stared at the video and the news accounts that followed. "This is youngin right here?! *Coldhearted?*" Tate inquired.

"That's him," Deuce affirmed from the backseat. Tate sat in the front passenger seat. "It's a rumor his adopted parents died in a fire. So, he got a lawsuit and a house and shit."

"Holy shit!" Tate laughed not because it was funny but astounding. "*GOD!!*" he exclaimed. "And now ... he carries that machete... *This* nygga!"

Deuce said quickly, "Here he come."

But Tate didn't care. "Ayo, homie. This is where you come from, huhn? What you lived through?"

Coldhearted buckled up and drove off. "You see it."

"Yeah, Deuce..." Tate said impressed nodding. "This a

boss nygga we fuckin' wit'. The official and I'm callin' it. We following *him!*"

"I respect dat, my nygga," Coldhearted told him, giving him some dap. When they were back in front of where Deuce lived both he and Tate got out.

"Stop by *Garter's* after twelve noon," Coldhearted told them. "You need to start on that rental unit plan so I'll bring you a package tomorrow."

With that they departed and Coldhearted drove home.

Chapter Thirty-Four

Taizhan & Rock
Garters Strip Club
Mt. Vernon, New York
Midnight

Taizhan was inside of the upstairs private office at *Garters* strip club. She was dressed in an all-white leather Gucci one-piece dress, she wore silver Chloe glasses and held a glass of Möet in her hand. Her feet were bare, those long pretty legs of hers were curled up beneath her as she relaxed on the large black leather crescent-shaped sofa. She could see both the VIP level upstairs and the entire downstairs where there were two stages, a long rectangular bar, rows of tables, strip poles and the staff wore white and black uniforms. It was a packed night a live DeeJay was tearing it up so the club was popping.

Rock was across the room sitting behind his desk talking to two near nude strippers who brought their grievances to him. He had sat there listening

to them for ten minutes.

"Here's the problem, Sierra," Desiree, a thick little light skinned babe From the Bronx, was saying. "Y'all bitches is taking these dudes to the Blue Rooms for "private dances" and taking bullshit twenty dollar tips for a head job. And when we take dudes back there they expecting sex for twenty dollars! Y'all thirsty hoes is fuckin' up the flow for real bitches cuz y'all giving it up for cheap!"

"Aight," Rock intervened in the dispute after hearing from both women. "Personally, Sierra, you too fuckin' cute to be even be givin' a handjob off for a funky ass dub."

Sierra, a badass white girl from the Bronx, also shook her head and sucked her teeth. "It ain't even always like that, Rock. I-"

"It should *never* be like that," Rock stated. "And from now on, to keep shit fair for all the girls who hustle ass on the side, there's gon' be *set* prices. If a mufucka wanna nut fifty for head, a hundred for pussy. Keep it simple. If they want multiple women the prices go up double, triple, yada, yada."

Sierra shrugged, indignant. "Next thing she'll be up here complaining about is we suck dick better. Then what?"

Rock laughed. "I can't help with that. Y'all go ahead. I'll tell the managers to enforce it."

The two strippers exited the office and the six feet four inch chocolate Rock rose up from behind his desk and locked the door. Taizhan peered over at him and couldn't help but smile.

Despite her twisted assignment by the Almighty Black P. Stones' Blood Bugout to spy on the Savage Hoodz boss and their organization, she had broken the cardinal rule of getting her feelings involved with "marks" that Bugout had sent her out on missions to spy on or even set up to be robbed or killed. She had never been ordered to kill anyone but she'd been involved in a list of terrifying and brutal crimes he'd commited in the past.

"You lookin' all good tonight," he said as he sat to her left. He reached out and traced a finger down her exposed leg. "Skin all soft and smooth. Feet pretty..."

She uncurled her legs and put her feet in his lap. She leaned back against the arm rest and ran her soft toes along the side of his face and ear. He caught her left ankle and kissed it. She put her toes playfully against his nose and he was instantly turned on. She had the prettiest feet he'd ever seen on a woman.

He sucked them cute toes one by one, slavering his tongue in between each one. She loved how he showed so much attention to her feet and how responsive he was to every part of her sweet body. Bugout was a brute and a freak -

it actually turned him on to hear of who and how she sucked and fucked other men. However, it disgusted and turned her on as well. But what she deeply hated was the physical abuse Bugout doled out on her. Especially when he'd hit her in her face.

As Rock literally worshipped her feet she could feel the honey-like cream escape from her pulsating vagina. She had no panties on so she knew that she would soon become moist between her buttocks and thighs and he'd smell her juicy scent.

"Every time you do that..." She started but stopped.

"Whatchu mean, baby?" he asked.

"You just love and appreciate me," she explained. "You're so protective of me. You kiss me like you miss me. Like I'm your wife and girlfriend. You are so kind to me. You foreplay with me and think of my pleasure first."

She pulled her feet away and sat up. She climbed up on top of him, sitting in his lap. She removed his tie and the white button-up shirt he wore, leaving only a white wife-beater under it. She ran her fingers through his hair, kissing him, smelling his awesome cologne and manly scent together. He wrapped his hands around her, feeling her from the legs all the way over her ass, back, and shoulders. She knew he loved her.

"I need you to be my woman," he said, holding her angelic face in his hands, peering deeply into those eerie gray eyes of hers. He kissed her full pink pillowy lips. "Just say it and know that I said I *need* you to be my woman. And I swear there's nothin' I wouldn't do for you, baby."

She looked down at him, her insides melting for him. "Swear it again. *Anything.* Say it and mean it."

"*Anything*," he emphasized. "Anything you want. Anything you need."

"Okay..." she murmured. "Sign the Viper over to me."

"That's it?" he asked, kissing her.

"Umm... I need twenty five grand."

"In the safe over there," he said. "C'mon, be serious."

She sat up straight. "Murder."

He stared at her. "C'mon now. Ask me something you really want or need. The car ain't much. The money ain't nothin'. Murder ain't shit."

"This one is," she said, "Caressing his chest and pulling off his wife-beater."

She took off her dress and he realized she'd been naked under it all evening. She went down to her knees to help him take off his shoes and slacks. She also took off his socks and boxers, leaving them both completely naked on the enormous leather sectional. The office was sufficiently sound-proofed against the booming music coming from the club but not 100%.

She pushed him onto his back and climbed on top of him. She laid down on him and the sexy couple touched, caressed let each other's hearts pound like drums together. Both of them were intensely aroused but in no rush. She could feel his hardened organ laying flat between them, pumping powerfully against her soft belly. He had always felt that there could be someone in her life that she was afraid of... although she had told him months earlier that she was single. He'd wanted to know but he didn't want to push her away. Was he an ex-husband? A maniac ex-boyfriend?

"Hey," he whispered. "Look at me."

She looked at him, eye to eye.

"Murder's no game," he said to her. "And I've killed before. If this needs done I'll do it. I said *anything*."

She whimpered into his mouth as they shared a deep, sloppy, tongue kiss. She reached between them and slowly moisturized his entire shaft with her oozing cunt juices for several excruciating minutes. She inserted the mushroom-like glans into her warm tunnel and took half of his mighty shaft inside of her tight cavern.

"Yes, Daddy," she whined. "Yes, Daddy, I'll be your woman. I'll be the best woman you ever had! And I love you, baby."

She took all of him inside of her little slippery pussy and she rode that beautiful chocolate dick like a champ. She was panting and her lithe yellow body was soaked with streams of steamy sweat. He let her do her thing for at least twenty minutes or so. Every time she would cum she would bite his neck or shoulder and he would spank her wet asscheeks and trace his fingers over their connected genitals and her asshole until her juicy cum was over. He smelled his soaked fingers, rubbing them into his nose.

"The thought of me killin' a nygga for you got that lil pussy gushin' today, huhn?" He asked as he turned her onto her hands and knees. He had her watching the packed crowds through the two-way mirror/window as he hammered that Jamaican-Chinese pussy from the back. "That pussy get hot don't it? Imma. Kill. Dat nygga. For. You!" The wild scent of her pussy turned him into a madman.

She screamed as Rock slammed his gigantic dick in and out of her. She looked back at him and twerked her fine yellow ass back at him.

"Oh, god yessss!" she whined. "Fuck me! Fuck me, Rock. This your pussy! Can you smell it, Daddy? Huhn?"

It was too much for him seeing all that shiny black dick thrusting into all that yellow and sparkling pink wetness. His balls exploded and it felt like the cum came from all over. He nearly blacked out. So, did she.

"Aight," Rock panted afterward, scooping his woman up into his arms. "Who has to die?"

"Let's get outta here," she told him. "And I'll show you."

Fifteen minutes later they left the club.

Chapter Thirty-Five

The Phantom House,
Danbury, Connecticut
2:40 AM

They drove north of the Hutchinson Parkway until they got to Danbury Connecticut. On the way there she explained to him how she was being relentlessly beaten by her father in law and blackmailed at the same time.

"Father in law?" Rock asked as he drove his black Yukon up through the quiet streets of Danbury.

"My sister married into this affluent Black family," Taizhan informed him. "I'm not proud of it but I've been or had been havin' an affair with her husband's father. He paid for college, bought me a Mercedes, a hundred thousand dollar condo, and gave me a Black Card."

Rock looked over at her. "I ain't judgin' you. You found a sucka and milked 'im. The drama is that the nygga is ya father in law."

She nodded. "I kept feelin' shame so I tried to end it. When I told him it was over he beat me and threatened to kill me. If my family ever finds out what I've done... I

just could not live with that."

"So, you showin' me where this mufucka lives," Rock said as she directed him to turn a right onto Mulberry Court.

"He's in Canada right now," she revealed. "But where we're goin' is to the house where... we rendezvous at. He leased it nearly a year ago."

Rock pulled up into a driveway and parked in front of one of the most beautiful mansions he'd ever seen. She opened up her purse and took out a garage door opener. She pressed the button and the garage door swung open.

"And you sure no one else is here?" Rock asked her.

She shook her head and showed him her smartphone. "God no! Only he and I ever come here so there's no risk of bein' caught by people who know us. This is the alarm system. No one disabled it so the house is ours. Lemme show you how to creep in, disable the alarm, where to hide, etcetera. So, when the moment comes - *pow*! and he's dead meat."

Rock didn't pull the truck into the garage. He just hopped out and looked around. It was dark out because the wee hours of the morning were not far off. There was a dewey-like floral fragrance in the night air. The only light came from the motion detector light in the driveway and from inside the garage. The garage lights came on

automatically once the garage door opened.

Rock packed a 9mm Beretta in a holster he had strapped to his belt. But he saw no reason in drawing the weapon. All was quiet and he was following his girl into her and her lover's love nest, so he had no need to be on heightened alert.

She walked him through the luxurious mansion and he was definitely looking at her in a different light. *This bitch is more than a exotic bombshell,* he thought. *She was treacherous, dangerous and James Bond movie bad. To fuck her sister's husband's father took some bravery and some cold blood.* But none of that mattered because Rock knew he had the hardest bitch ever now. And all he had to do to solidify their union was kill one person? That would be too easy.

He checked out the entire premises and they exited with a plan in mind. They spoke about it on the way to Croton On The Hudson where he dropped her off at her building. She kissed him goodbye and went inside.

Rock drove back to Mt. Vernon, wondering how much money they pulled in the previous evening. He felt on top of the world. He texted Chubby that he was nearby and on his way. He also texted his mother a *"GoodMorning!"*

Then, as he sat at a red light about half a mile from *Garters,* a black van drove up alongside him with a brown skinned woman driving. He could see her lighting up a cigarette as she waited for the light to turn green. Suddenly the side doors opened and two men jumped out and had AR-15's trained on Rock.

BBBRAAAATTT!!! Machine gun blasts!

BB- R-RAAATTT! Rock never had a chance!

Caught by surprise the lethal bullets ripped through the doors and windows and into Rock's side, arm, neck and cheek in seconds! The rapid bursts of firepower woke up the entire neighborhood! And just like that the two masked men leaped back into the van and it sped away.

Rock's Yukon rolled out into the intersection and came to a stop directly in the center of it. He lay dead with his face across the steering wheel.

MEANWHILE, as Taizhan sat at her vanity inside of the bedroom she shared with Bugout, she slowly used make-up removal pads to wipe the eyeliner from her amazing almond-like eyes. Bugout laid up against the pillows with a red silk robe on. He was smoking a blunt and eyeing Taizhan.

When his phone rang she got up to retrieve it from the dresser where he'd left it. She recognized the caller ID name: "ASIA" which was the woman who'd been driving the van with the hittaz inside of it. The call was actually a text which read: *"Rock was killed."* Bugout showed it to Taizhan. "You did excellent work," he congratulated her. "Your loyalty will be rewarded."

Seconds later Bugout's phone rang. This time it was a call from an unknown number. Probably a burner phone.

"Yeah," Bugout answered.

"I love when a plan comes together," Almighty Black P. Stones leader P-Man said.

"That's right," Bugout said.

"Y'all stay up," P-man told them. "Stay off the streets. We ain't done yet."

Taizhan saw Bugout sit the phone aside and open his robe up to reveal how stiff

and hot he was. "C'mon, baby. You know what I need," he encouraged her to fellate him. As she took him into her mouth tears flowed from her eyes. Her heart had gotten wrapped up in Rock and he'd truly loved her... Taizhan was crying because she had killed that love.

Chapter Thirty-Six

Word of Rock's Murder

Mt. Vernon, NY

The club had cleared out by 4:00 AM except for Savage Hoodz members and a large group mixed with Garters security and Crips who were in the back room shooting dice. One of the SHZ Girlz, Ava Applez shot a group text to everyone in the crew that Rock had been shot.

"Everybody out!" Tommy Gunz yelled. "Guns up! Let's roll out!"

Chubb, Dojo, HK, Mac-11, Shadow, Choir Boy, Wolfman, Orca, Sonja, Alejandra, Shay, Joyce, Blue Eyes, and

Juicy were all there. Tate, Deuce, Double J, Spooky and a whole mob of Neighborhood Crips were back there as well. Tommy Gunz locked up the back and front door's before bolting up the street to Connor Avenue and Heath Boulevard where there was already one police car and incoming sirens from more first responders.

The SHZ and Crips stayed frosty behind the yellow tape the officer had put up. Chubb slid his gun to Bhad Barbie and, went out to the street to talk to the dark haired police officer.

"Stay on the other side of the tape, son," the officer ordered Chubb. "Are you a family member?"

Chubb nodded as three more squad cars arrived. Juicy P was hugging Ava Applez and crying.

The officer allowed Chubby to have a quick look at Rock's body since Chubby had told him that he was Rock's brother. So, the officer with the big nose and dark hair pulled back the tarp that covered the car and Chubby, tears in his eyes, nodded.

"Yes, sir, that's him," Chubby cried, unable to hold it in.

The fire department, ambulance and a coroner's van pulled up. The office had Chubby sit in the front of his police car. He knew the homicide detectives would eventually be there and would want to interview him. Chubby called his mother, Tanya Taylor, just, as the shiny new grill of Coldhearted's Cadillac truck pulled up at the corner.

Coldhearted got out of the passenger's side with Liza on

his heels as they made their way over to the SHZ and Crip mob across the street.

"What da fuck happened?" Liza demanded.

Ava Applez answered. "Rock was mowed down. Chubb's in the squad car over there cuz he's his lil' brother. I was leavin' the club to go home and heard the gunshots. So, I drove up here, seen the blood on the windows, and texted everybody."

Liza held her stomach. She turned to look for Cold-hearted. He was quiet and had nothing to say as Liza turned her back to him which caused him to pull her up against his body. She loved how he staked his claim on her as if she was gold or something. He made her feel *possessed* and *owned* which her chicas in the Bronx spoke negatively about.

"*No man, should own you,*" her homegirl Rita told her. "*or control you.*"

"*You should live free,*" another friend named Franny had urged her. "*You ever hear the word libertad?*"

But she'd brush them off. Sage and Liza were inseparable. They were incredible friends and though they still had a lot to learn they were blessed to be so intelligent and so in love. Liza never thought for one second that her possessive and obsessive feelings for her daughter's father were unhealthy. And, vice versa. They belonged to each other.

Right now, Liza was more worried about what was going to happen now that Rock had been assassinated, they stood there for nearly two hours before Rock's bullet-riddled body was taken out of the SUV, laid onto a stretcher, and zipped up inside of a burgundy bodybag. He was carted over to the coroner's van and placed into the back. Angry and sad tears flowed down nearly all of the SHZ and SHZ Girlz' faces.

When they put the Yukon up onto a flatbed truck all of the SHZ clan got a clear look at all of the bullets that had ripped through the driver's side.

"Yeah, this was a set up," Coldhearted said as he stood on the edge of the sidewalk. "All the entries came from the driver's side. They pulled up in somethin' and ambushed him. They had to follow him from somewhere... *Taizhan*. Who was he wit last night? The Chinese Black girl? Taizhan?"

Tommy Gunz nodded. "Wit her. He slid out wit her maybe midnightish or later. I seen 'em leave. He usually takes her home up Croton."

Coldhearted had the look of death in his eyes as he turned to his crew. "This was no random hit. This was a Blood hit because we takin' all this street money in now. Rock's death was a message for us to shut down shop. Well we ain't shutting down shit. Right?"

Tommy Gunz nodded. "Fuckin' right."

Orca agreed.

Shadow joined in.

The SHZ Girlz vowed to fight.

"It's gunz up, mufuckaz," Tommy said.

"Yeah, we got plenty of those," Coldhearted said, staring

at Rock's Yukon being driven away. He felt the machete sheathed under his hoody sweatshirt in the back. "Y'all can have all the guns y'all want. I have what I need."

The entire crew knew exactly what he meant. The crazy mufucka carried it strapped to his back in a fancy black alligator leather sheath. And he'd even given it a sinister name: HEARTLESS.

Coldhearted walked over to OG Bobby Tate and pulled him to the side with Tommy Gunz. "Y'all niggaz ready?"

"Born ready, son," Tommy growled, anger in his voice.

Bobby Tate was down 100%. "Let's do it."

Coldhearted slapped him on the arm. "War's been declared and we accept. We Bloodhunters now, kid."

Part Three

"Out For Blood"

Quote

I am going to be famous one day... but it'll be for all the wrong reasons.
reasons.
Anthony Sowell (Ohio Serial Killer)

Chapter Thirty-Seven

Taizhan & Coldhearted
Mt. Vernon Police Dept.

On their way home Coldhearted drove the sleek charcoal black Cadillac SUV with the ghost finish. Liza sat up front next to him, Chubb sat frozen in the back with Deuce and Tate who were silent and caught up in their own thoughts.

Just as they stopped outside of Chubb's mother's house Coldhearted received a phone call from Taizhan.

"Boys, it's that bitch Rock was wit," Coldhearted said, waving the phone around.

"Play it by ear, C," Tate instructed him. "Everyone quiet. Speakerphone, homie."

"Hello?" C said.

"Is it true?" Taizhan queried in a small, quivering voice. "Is he gone?"

Coldhearted sat back in the driver's seat. "Whatchu – watchin' the news?"

"No." She could be heard crying, trying to contain herself. "The police called me. They said they were told I was with him last night."

They almost had trouble making out her words through the sobs.

"Where are you?" Coldhearted asked her.

"In Croton," She sniffled. "On my way to the Mount Vernon Police Department... they wanna question me."

Silence.

"What happened?" she questioned Coldhearted.

"You ain't see the news?"

"No!" she cried. "He brought me home after we drove up to Connecticut. And as soon as I'm out the shower and in the bed the cops call... what happened to, him?"

Coldhearted looked back at Chubb and Tate.

Tate nodded.

"Nyggas shot 'im up," Coldhearted answered.

They heard her yelp and break down.

Coldhearted looked at Liza and saw that she had turned

red around her ears and nose before crying herself. He knew then that his own chick believed Taizhan.

Moments later Taizhan spoke again. "He just asked me if I'd be his woman! We were in love... oh my god Imma be sick."

They could literally hear her vomiting. Then a toilet was flushing and a sink running.

"Can you pick me up?" Taizhan asked Coldhearted a minute later. "I can't drive like this."

Coldhearted looked at Liza. "I don't even know Corton. But I'll send someone up there to get you."

A short pause. Then she said, "That's okay. I'll call a car."

Liza motioned for him to take the phone off of Speakerphone.

"Hold on Tay," he said, putting her on "HOLD"

"That's Rock's girl, man," Liza chided. "You hear she's in a million pieces and you makin' her take a cab to see the cops?"

Coldhearted took her off "HOLD." "Aight, Tay, tell me how to get there..."

She gave him directions as Chubb exited the vehicle. Coldhearted drove Liza home next. Tate and Deuce fell asleep in the back of the caddy as Coldhearted drove to pick up Taizhan.

She had directed him to a Getty gas station near her building. He pulled up next to a full-service gas pump and got out just as Taizhan walked up to the establishment.

"Fill it up wit' premium," Coldhearted told the Indian gas station attendant "Tay."

The exotic Chinese- Jamaican beauty approached him and he saw her bloodshot eyes. In an instant they were embracing one another and he felt her powerful sadness shaking her to the core. She was overcome with grief.

A few minutes later they were back in the vehicle, on their way to the police station.

When they got there they all went inside and were met by homicide detectives. They interviewed Taizhan for over an hour while Coldhearted, Tate, and Deuce

waited in a breakroom.

"She ain't have nuthin' to do wit that shit." Coldhearted said in a tired sigh.

Tate shrugged. "At this point everybody suspect. And if we don't hit back... we may as well pack it up."

"We all witchu on that," Coldhearted stated.

"Nyggas like these only understand one language," Tate stated wisely. "*Killin'*. Whatchu thinkin'?"

Coldhearted shook his head. "What's in my head is too sinister to talk about in a police station."

Chapter Thirty-Eight

Garters

After Funeral Party

The funeral was held ten days later at Adam's Funeral Home and the First Church of Our Lord Jesus Christ. There was no casket because Rock had been cremated. His family did not believe in the false capitalist assertion, of "Christian burial." Rock's mom, Tanya Taylor, had control of all of his hidden cash but she saw no reason in spending any of it on a lavish, senseless, burial in some cemetery.

Of course, the entire Savage Hoodz came out in full force. This included the SHZ Girlz, a lot of friends Rock had known all throughout his life and those people he'd gone to school with. Tanya and Rock's Father had invited all of their family members and friends.

Taizhan came with another young woman that nobody knew but she certainly drew an abundance of glances in her direction because she was so attractive. They also, looked related. The woman was Taizhan's nineteen year old half sister - also part Jamaican part Chinese. Her name was Seji and she was the color of cinnamon graham crackers, red hair, freckles on her beautiful face and big brown almond-shaped eyes. She sure was something to look at.

"I'm so fuckin' jealous," Liza whispered to Coldhearted as they chilled at Garters later in the evening to eat and have a private party for Rock's homegoing.

"Why?" he asked his girl.

"First Taizhan, now Seji," Liza stated. "They look stolen from God they're so *beautiful*! If I was a lesbian I'd want Seji. I'd *marry* her."

Taizhan overheard Liza and smiled. She was sitting at the next table with her back turned to Liza and Coldhearted. But Seji was seated where she could see them to the left. Taizhan quickly repeated what she'd heard Liza say.

Tommy called Coldhearted just then and he excused himself. "Gimme a minute babe," he said to her and walked off.

Seji stood up from her chair and slid into Coldhearted's seat. "Hi," Seji, chirped.

Liza smiled at the pretty red head. "Hi."

"I'm Seji," she introduced herself. "And I know you're Liza."

"Mm-hmm," Liza said nodding at the stunning young beauty.

"I kinda heard what you said about if you was a lesbian." Seji giggled all girlishly.

Liza flushed red with embarrassment. "Aw shit."

"No, don't be feel bad," Seji said. "I get it all the time... just not by the right kind of girl. If I'm ever gonna try it with a woman she has to have everything I like."

Liza looked confused. "I was sayin' how beautiful and exotic you and your sister was, I mean... I've never..."

Seji grabbed Liza's hand. "Me neither. No offense. I was sittin' there thinkin' the same thing about you. You're Latina, long hair, a beautiful face and... fat ass, even through that dress. I'm just sayin'... I'm new in town. You get a free moment... call me. Let's be each other's secret because my family is too religious.

She wrote down her phone number and went back to her table. Five minutes later Coldhearted returned.

"What's up, mami?" he asked.

Liza looked up at him and shook her head. "Nothin'."

She put the number into her purse and couldn't help but to think about what the exotic sister had said to her. Liza stared at her man.

"Can we go home?" she asked him, reaching under the

table and running her hand lovingly along the shaft of his meat.

He looked at her funny. "You horny after a funeral?"

She shrugged. "Is that weird?"

"We gotta stay," he told her, glancing at his watch.

"Why?" she whimpered sexily into his ear, moving closer, to him. "Daddy my clit is thumping mad wild right now."

She rubbed him making him to tent in his dress slacks. He squirmed underneath her caresses.

"We need an alibi, baby," he whispered. "And it's cameras all around."

"Mm, alibi?"

He nodded and kissed her pink lips. "Nyggas is about to die... Why yo stuff so turned on?"

She smiled shyly, licking his ear. "I don't have panties on or nuttin'."

He frowned. "So? You never have no panties on unless you walkin' around Lilly in the crib. You hot for somethin'."

"That red head girl," she whispered in his ear.

Coldhearted was surprised. "Word? We be in here around all these nekkid bitches all the time... and you never acted like that."

"You don't like it?"

"I ain't say that," he said quickly, looking over at the exotic light skinned almond-eyes red head. "I mean... *look* at her. I can see why."

"I'm not gay," she said and shrugged. "But every female

has a crush or fantasizes about another bitch sometimes. For that bitch right there...? My pussy is steamy right now."

Seji was most certainly betwitching. She and Taizhan had that effect on many people – men and women.

"Damn," Coldhearted stated. "You wanna fuck her?"

Liza softly stroked his engorged phallus under the table. "Look how turned on you are by the thought of seein' me and her makin' love... Take me in the office and fuck me Sage."

He stood up and pulled her along with him.

Chapter Thirty-Nine

The Triple Car Bombings
8:45 PM
Mt. Vernon, NY

Bugout sat at the glass table across from his capo Blood Nimrod and his lieutenant Blood Bain. All three men were smoking weed and counting out money. There were ten other Bronx Black P. Stones inside of the stash pad.

"This is a lot of fuckin' twenties, Blood." Bugout complained as he stood up.

Out in the living room the music was rocking to an upbeat Usher song and the six girls were out there seeing who could dance the best. Bugout lifted the heavy black canvas duffel bag over his shoulder and, hearing the girls squealing with excitement, he stood at the door – watching them.

One short dark skinned pretty little thing named Daysia was going hard. She had on a cute white Fendi dress and Air Max's. She had to pull the dress up high on her knees to twerk. When she noticed Bugout, Bain and Nimrod observing she went buck wild, laying almost flat on the floor and doing a "twerk-twirl" that had every man in the room fascinated. Another girl, Shonette, reached down and pulled Daysia's dress up over her bouncing buttcheeks. Daysia had on high-riding pink boyshorts which showed off the tattoos on her buttocks and the backs of her thighs. Her ass is precisely why nyggaz put they faces between bad bitches booties and why we suck and lick they cute little anuses, Bugout was thinking why bitches love doin' that shit to us men... I'll never know.

"Who's shorty?" Bugout inquired to Nimrod.

Nimrob shrugged. "She work at The Clover bar over there on Houston Steet and Market."

"She a bottle girl?" Bugout asked.

Nimrod nodded. "Her name Day-Day."

Bugout waited for her to finish dancing before whispering in her ear. As he did she was reaching underneath her dress to pull her boyshorts out of her pussy and asscrack.

"Mm, you so nasty," Daysia said back to him as she panted, out of breath. "Plus I'm mad sweaty right now..."

"That's what a bubble bath at the Bancroft is for girl," he said, his 5 foot 11 inch tall height towering over her 5 feet even stature. "C'mon."

"He takin' you to da *Bancroft*?!" Shonette whispered to her friend. "That hotel is *Paradise!*"

Daysia grabbed her things, a small purse and a jacket, and walked up to Bugout. She'd never slept with him before but all the girls who hung out around the P. Stones knew that fucking the boss came with perks.

"Go get ya car and bring it around back," Bugout told her.

He had notoriously bad breath and she nearly choked when he spoke to her. But she just nodded and walked away. She waved goodbye to her friends and left out the front door to go up the block and retrieve her car.

"He fine and all but damn..." the cute little Hershey's chocolate kiss whispered as she hurried down the front steps and up the street to her burgundy Honda Accord. "His breath! That nygga need to brush his fuckin' throat out with bleach or somethin'. Damn!"

But, as she drove her car around back, she was thinking of the bills Bugout could pay and the material luxuries he could provide. When she got behind the wheel and started the car she noticed – or thought she noticed – someone watching her from the rear of a Verizon van.

Part of her dismissed it but as she drove past the van, she expected to see a Verizon worker sitting up front but she saw no one. Thinking she was just tripping she just kept it moving.

Inside of the Verizon van were OG Bobby Tate, Tommy Gunz, and Shadow Warrior. The OG Rollin' 60s Neighborhood Crip quietly eyed the Honda and the fine dark skinned babe as she drove past their Verizon van. Of course, he had no way of knowing that she was about to pick up the local Almighty Black P. Stone boss Blood Bugout in the alley in back of the house.

"Time to move!" Tate ordered as the three of the men hopped out of the side door of the van.

Each of them held percussion grenade launchers in their hands. They wore Verizon worker uniforms, baseballccaps and demon masks as they ran up to the house and launched the grenades in through the front windows of the residence!

At that very moment, however, Bugout was already inside of Daysia's car and they were on the move with $1000s of dollars of P. Stone drug money.

Out front, Bobby Tate, Tommy Gunz and 18 year old Shadow Warrior were back inside of the Verizon van. Tate drove off and parked around the corner.

They waited for the men, and some of the women to come running out of the house which they did! And just as Tate and his boys had anticipated the occuoants of the house ended up heading to several cars parked out on the street, scattering like roaches from the hell that had come down on them!

But they hadn't seen anything yet!

Once they were inside of their vehicles... that's when the party started. Four Bloods inside of a green Acura, two more males and three females inside of a Toyota 4Runner. Blood Bain and Blood Nimrod inside of a red Mercedes. Each of them unaware that they'd been hunted for a week going in and out of a well-known Blood member hangout. Hunted by real gangster Crips from L.A. to New York by Coldhearted.

The triple blasts were spread out over a one to two block radius, to the ditances where they three cars had made it to after they'd fled. The sounds of the explosions, however, could be heard for more than a mile!

Minutes later the three men were removing the ficticious magnetic signs and decals they had affixed to the sides of the utility van the previous day. They also removed the false license plates, their demon masks and Verizon worker uniforms which were all placed into a black garbage bag.

"Aight let's move!" Tate ordered.

They jumped back into the van and drove away from the abandoned carwash. They headed out to the Savage Hoodz HQ where the van was safely and clandestinely destroyed with the bag and percussion grenade launchers.

Behind the SHZ HQ lofts was a gravel field where the van burned to a crisp while the killer trio sat on the rooftop looking out. But on this industrial edge of town they knew that they could burn just about anything with no interference as long as it wasn't anything too great.

OG Bobby Tate lit up a cigarette and passed the pack to Tommy.

Shadow Warrior pulled out a burner phone and put in the call to Coldhearted.

He answered, out of breath. "Yeah."

"Boom, boom, boom," Shadow said.

The line went dead.

Shadow looked over at the van and said, "That bitched burned out, son. Let's ride."

The trio made their way out into the front parking lot and inside one of the many leased luxury vehicles Rock had had on deck for SHZ. It was an all gold Lincoln Navigator.

"Yeah, nyggas," Tate said as he peeled off his New York Yankees fitted cap back. "This nygga Coldhearted is dead serious!"

"Whatchu mean?" Shadow inquired.

"I can't believe them bombs he gave us to plant even worked!" Tate emitted a dark laugh. "Well – it's the game of death now, homie!"

Tommy and Shadow nodded.

Chapter Forty

On-Scene Investigators
The P. Stone Massacre
10:00 PM
Mt. Vernon, NY

Police were swarming the Mt. Vernon neighborhood like bees. Bomb squad units had already converged and cleared over eighty-plus cars that were parked in the area. The Mt. Vernon Police Department, Fire Department and EMS-Ambulances were being assisted by other agencies as well. Among these were first responders from neighboring Pelham, New Rochelle and NYPD (Bronx).

"This is a goddamned shit show!" Sergeant John Holland

remarked as he and several law enforcement officers peered closely into the bombed out red Mercedes that was driven by Bain with Nimrod ridin' shotgun. "We have two deceased here."

One of the bomb squad technicians was looking around on the street with a powerful flashlight when ATF agents showed up. Sergeant Holland of the MVPD was in charge of the scene until the ATF and FBI arrived and took over.

"Check this, Sarge," a bomb tech called out to him.

The bomb expert's name was George Macon of the Mt. Vernon Police Department's Bomb Unit.

"Whatcha got, Macon?" Sergant Holland answered as he approached.

Macon, a veteran of the Army Rangers, help up a burn out piece of metal and plastic. "Anyone know what this is?" he asked.

Sergeant Holland, surrounded by a group of other officers and federal agents, shook his head. "What is it?" Holland queried.

"A fuckin' mercury switch," Macon replied. "I seen these in Afghanistan... UBL used them. Whoever made these devices are scary."

The FBI and ATF agents gathered together to dicuss where the bomb component evidence would be analyzed. The ATF decided to analyze 50% of the evidence collected at their New York agency in White Plains.

"These cars are registered to known Piru gang members,

"FBI Special Agent Jim Mulligan reported to Sergeant Holland. "Any gang members livin' aournd here, Sergeant?"

"Right around the corner there's a so-called gang hang-out... 1536 Laramie," the sergeant pointed over a row of houses in a direction a block away from where they were standing. "Our narcotics officers have spoke about the house as being used to host what they hear are loud parties where drugs are being used. They've tried to send CI's in there but to no avail. The Almighty Black P. Stones own most of Mt. Vernon, especially south Mt. Vernon. We believe the Laramie Street hangout is for the enforcers to protect their crown jewel traphouse around the corner on Jarret Avenue."

The bomb squad responded to 1536 Laramie Street and shined a light on the front of the house. They knocked but by now the house was empty. The bomb squad breached the front door, cleared each room of the house first and a forensic team entered.

"Whattawegot out there eleven victims?" Sergeant asked anyone who was listening.

"Yeah Sarge," a CSI officer answered as they walked through the house.

Sergeant Holland bent down and picked up an empty percussion grenade. "They were specifically targeting the Blood gang. This is how they got 'em to run out of the house... and to their cars where the bombs were already planted."

FBI Special Agent Mulligam said, "The unsubs, or unknown subjects, likely set out to assassinate this group.

They managed to get the bombs secured while the victims were unaware, in here partying. And the percussion devices flushed them right out to their death."

Sergeant Holland turned to the patrol officer and ordered him to do some footwork. "Get a team of 10 officers together and do a canvas. We need any traffic pods in the area... Private cell phone, or doorbell cameras - collect all youse can."

There had to be hundreds - or perhaps even over a thousand - of bewildered spectators and neighborhood residents observing the heavy police and federal response. Among the spectators was Bugout who watched what remained of the red Mercedes as it was driven off on a flatbed truck. He had already received confirmation that his closest men – Nimrod and Bain – were inside of the car during the explosion.

Bugout and Daysia had *just* driven off when they'd heard the three blasts. They had looped around the block to see what they could see at the time and they'd seen the carnage. The green Acura blown up, on fire. The 4Runner with the five burnt bodies inside of it and by that time Bugout had had Daysia take him home so he could put the duffel bag full of money in the safe.

"C'mon, baby," Bugout told Daysia who was still with him.

"Where to now?" she asked him when they were inside of her car.

"You know where Garters is at?"

"Who *don't* know where Garters is at?" she said back. "It's that strip joint up on Richlee."

He pulled out a stack of cash. "I expect you to never repeat nothin' you hear or see when it comes to me, my business, my nyggaz, my bitches, my money, nothin – ya heard?"

"I know da rules, Daddy," she said, feeding his ego.

He dropped $500 on her lap and she drove to Garters as he instructed.

Chapter Forty-One

Garters

Mt. Vernon, NY

11:00 PM

"**I**'m tellin' you, Bugout, they're all here!" Taizhan assured him. "No one left since the funeral came to the party."

He paused. She could hear the way that he was breathing that he was both enraged and paranoid. Anyone who knew Bugout he was a real live "730" nygga- hence the name "Bugout." He wasn't afraid of nothing, nobody or anything. He smoked "K2 Dippers," popped zannies, perks and adderal. Plus, he was a paranoid schitzophrenic killer with a high body count.

"I'm fuckin' coming in to see for myself," Bugout growled into the phone.

Inside, Taizhan put her phone away and tried not to look nervous. "Oh my god," she muttered.

Her half sister, Seji, who was buzzing and feeling real good off of the expensive drinks she'd been tossing back, looked at Taizhan quizzically. "What?" she asked.

"Bugout 'bout to come in here!" Taizhan whispered.

"What!?" Seji whispered back. "We handlin' this! Why?"

"Three car bombs went off and a bunch of people dead down on Laramie," Taizhan revealed, trying to let the news sink in through her alcohol-fueled haze. "I think he said eleven people."

Seji put her hand over her heart as though it hurt or as if she were having a panic attack. "So, he thinks these nyggaz hit back..."

Just then Bugout walked in and he was not alone. He had made a phone call and now he was mobbin' in something like fourteen hardcore Almighty Black P. Stone. These cats weren't no ordinary dudes either. They were all goons that stood six feet tall 250 pounds and better.

The club was flooded with all the SHZ men and women. Plus, there were well over 200 rolling 60s Crips, and dozens of strippers and other club personnel. The funeral party was now a full-fledged sorry, wide open to the public. Coldhearted had given the word to the head of security to let everyone inside.

From where Coldhearted sat with Liza, Tate, Tommy Gunz, Shadow Warrior, and Deuce, they could see whoever came through the front door's downstairs. It was a perk of VIP. Plus, the "H.O.S." or head of security, had already alerted Coldhearted and Tommy Gunz that they had visitors asking for the "New Savage Hoodz boss."

"These nyggas is lookin' for the new Savage Hoodz boss, son," Coldhearted showed Tommy the text he was sent by the H.O.S.

Coldhearted stood up and walked off. He was followed by Tommy downstairs when the now 19 year old, 5 foot 10 inch, co-owner of Garters stopped Coldhearted.

"Son," Tommy said, scratching in between his cornrows thoughtfully. "*Who is* the boss of the SHZ empire now?"

Coldhearted had been worn by Liza, Tate and Deuce that Tommy might want the top spot within SHZ Inc which included Savage Hoodz Records, the club, and more. However, Coldhearted was part owner of Garters... And, deep down, he wanted it all. The problem was that he and Tommy were still underage and could not own a liquor license. Tanya Taylor - Rock and Chubb's mother - was the silent partner of SHZ Inc. and it was *she* that held those documents.

Coldhearted knew he could mount a sinister and violent takeover of the business but that wouldn't be smart right now.

He had the strength and respect of the entire SHZ gang and the Rollin 60s Neighborhood Crips. The Crips would kidnap Tommy, Chubb, Tonya and everyone they were connected to if Coldhearted gave the order. These were things he actually spoke about out loud to the two cats he started to trust more than anyone inside of SHZ. OG Bobby Tate and Deuce.

"I'd killed Tommy, Chubb, Tanya - any of them in order to take over the club and record company," Coldhearted had confided to them. "My whole time with this crew... they soft, son. A few of 'em will bust the blicky... but I see the fear in their faces. I'm a nygga who has no problem with looking at mark in the eye and killing 'em with my bare hands."

"Miss Heartless," Deuce had laughed.

Coldhearted had pulled out his gleaming machete nickname "Heartless" from the expensive black $3000 alligator skin scabbard holstered to his back. "Yep. My baby... Now, what y'all think?"

Tate had laid it all out. "I know someone who knows how to make bombs. But the business right now. Focus on monstering out the monster first: taking over this territory. And we do it with the boom not bullets, not a machete."

Coldhearted had thought about it. "And y'all call me the evil genius. Tell me how to do it."

Tate had shook his head no. "Leave it to me. By any means I have to leave SHZ out of it... I may need one man. Give me Tommy so his hands is deep in it. No one else becuz the feds are gonna rain down on this shit like a waterfall.

Presently, Coldhearted stood in the VIP stairwell with Tommy and told him, "Look son, you and me own Garters now with Tanya as the silent partner over SHZ Inc. For this mufucka and or any other who need to know... it's a Tommy and Coldhearted show. We da fuckin' bosses."

Tommy didn't even have the chance to reply because Coldhearted turned and walked on downstairs. Tommy followed him. Upstairs, in VIP, Tate observed what was going on and told Deuce to send a Crip brigade down there with them.

"I'm sure they ain't get through security with weapons," Tate said, watching.

"I got it," Duece said and tapped several of the big Crip homies on the shoulder. "Neighborhood!" He yelled out.

In a second, a mob of Crips were on their feet following Deuce's war cry. "Neighborhood!" They all called out.

Taizhan, Seji, and Liza all sat with their mouths open as something like 35 Crips left the VIP to go downstairs.

Chapter Forty-Two

Garters

Mt. Vernon, NY

Liza stood by OG Bobby Tate and asked him, "What's gonna happen? Cuz my kid is at home and I don't need to get caught up in this shit."

"You good," Tate calmed her as Seji and Taizhan walked over to the two-way glass overlooking the floor below. Just let them handle it."

There was a wide open island bar on the main floor of the club. All around the open air bar, in a 360 degree angle, where tables and private booths, two stages, a live Deejay, dozens of near-nude girls working hard for their green in a capacity crowd.

Bugout and his men were scanning the club with their backs toward the bar, waiting. Tommy walked directly up to the 31 year old, 5 foot 11 inch tall thug with all the Blood tattoos covering his face and neck like an anatomical landscape.

"I'm Tommy Gunz," Tommy introduced himself. "And this is my partner - we call him Coldhearted. We own Garters. How can we help you?"

Bugout eyed Tommy and Coldhearted, silently breathing hatred in and out of his nostrils. He also noticed the large mob of Crips who had encircled his own 15-man team. And right away the Almighty P. Stone gangster knew that Tommy and Coldhearted knew who he was. They never asked him his name.

"Well?" Tommy spread his arms.

"You mufuckas bombed my folks over on the southside," Bugout accused them.

Tommy looked like he was about to blow a gasket.

"What?!" Tommy snapped.

Coldhearted stepped in. "Y'all wanna do this right here?" He pointed a thumb at them at the large crowds.

Bugout glared at Tommy for a few moments and then at Coldhearted.

"C'mon, son," Coldhearted said to Tommy. "To the manager's office."

Bugout wanted facts so he followed them to the office. The fourteen Piru goons that came with Bugout stayed out in the hallway while over three dozen Rollin 60s killers did the same. Young boy Deuce, who despised Bloods was ready to go to war. All the Crips were already armed up and they knew the P. Stones had been searched coming in. It would be a slaughter because the Bloods had no weapons.

Coldhearted put the Channel 2 news on the Internet and there it was. The bombings, the heavy police presence, bodies being pulled out of the cars and placed into body bags.

"First we heard of it," Coldhearted said to Bugout. "Nobody in our funeral party left until dinner was over and we opened up the front doors."

"I'll never believe y'all ain't have nothing to do with killing my closest men," Bugout blamed Coldhearted as he stared him squarely in the eye. "Who was it? Y'all had to bring nem in from out of town."

"Why?" Tommy asked gruffly. "Because you had rock murdered? Now you think we retaliated? Lemme tell you somethin'..."

Tommy walked up to the older man. "I deal death in bullets not bombs."

Bugout nodded, moving towards the door, watching as Coldhearted removed his machete from the scabbard on his back. "And I love the trusty machete. It runs in the family."

"The law will be over here," Tommy told Bugout. "And we all have alibis. The digital camera system here can pick up a roach moving. And we'll give all the alibi footage to the cops when they come. Can't be in two places at one time."

Bugout was about to leave when Coldhearted stopped him in the hallway. Coldhearted, holding *Miss Heartless* in his hand, came out into the hallway.

"You came to accuse *us*," Coldhearted said. "When you da one who busted on Rock. Now somethin' happen to you and you mad about it? How's it feel?"

Tommy wondered what the hell he was doing.

"So y'all did it?" Bugout said. "You admitting it?"

"I didn't say that. We denied that already," Coldhearted stated slowly. "Stop hearin' whatchu wanna hear, nygga, and listen! You bullied Rock on outta here like a tyrant. And now that the chickens have come home to roost youse mad. Why?"

Bugout refused to play the mind games this young nygga was playing. "Look nygga whoever the fuck you are. This is *my* territory and-"

"*Pause*," Coldhearted stopped him. "The name is Sage Michael Thomas. Do ya research on who I am and where I came from."

Bugout stared hard at the young buck. "Like I said. This is P. Stone territory and y'all trespassin'. This shit-"

"We ain't trying to hear it," Coldhearted waved him off. "Nobody owned shit. And them days of walkin' all over Savage Hoodz is finished. Y'all killed Rock but woke up the Kracken. I got 150 Rolling 60s out here holding me down to da death, nygga. and I can call in 200 more, military style weapons and all wit' 'em."

Bugout glared at him. "Bombs are a step up from murder, kid."

Coldhearted chuckled. "No one's admitting that. *You* keep pushin' that narrative."

Coldhearted, holding the machete at his side, walked up to Bugout and looked him directly in his eyes. "Allz I'm saying is... we in town, son, and we can be bullies too."

Bugout knew the conversation was over. He and his men exited the club.

Chapter Forty-Three

Liza & Coldhearted's House
Mt. Vernon, NY
11:30 AM

"Let's put the house up for sale," Coldhearted said the very next day to Liza.

Elizabeth had just served everyone at the table egg and sausage burritos and freshly squeezed orange juice. Lilly was happy she was being kept out of school for her 10th birthday.

Liza was feeding their daughter Isabel Maria Garcia Thomas chewed up burrito from out of her mouth. Isabel was one of those babies that refused her bottle when she saw everyone eating solid foods.

Double Deuce and his cousins - Double J and Spooky - now lived in the basement apartment. They had gotten permission from their mothers to do so once they had met Elizabeth. Coldhearted had wanted them there not only because he and Deuce had gotten so close but Deuce would vest up and ride like a soldier if danger came.

"And move where?" Elizabeth asked as Deuce, Double J and Spooky came from downstairs.

"We smelled this good shit," Spooky commented.

"Spooky! The kids, man," Elizabeth checked him.

"Sorry, Miss Elizabeth," the dark skinned fifteen year old apologized. He had his hair braided back in big corn rows to manage his long hair. "Sorry Lilly and baby Izzy."

"Y'all mama need y'all to come over," Liza told the three teens. She looked at her man. "So?"

"It's an emergency move," Coldhearted told Liza. "Find somethin' gated, mad security, doorman, gateman — all that shit. We gonna buy up. As in trade up? We upgrading, baby."

Liza wasn't so sure about that. "Man, this property was custom built after the fire. It's mad big yo. Put a wall up, beef up security, Lilly can home school."

"Yeah we can do that," he sighed. "But what about when one of them Piru cats see y'all at Pathmark or Target or the gas station?"

Elizabeth shook her head. "Y'all is too young to have all

this weight on your shoulders. I mean that club is an amazing asset you and your friends put together... thank God for Tanya getting behind Rock like she did. But all the other gang and street stuff, Sage..."

He looked up at her as she put more food on everyone's plate. They were killing those burritos. Even Isabel was reaching for her mama's mouth for more, making Coldhearted laugh.

"Will you chew up some more burrito for her greedy lil behind?" Coldhearted said to Liza. "She hungry as a mug."

He paused.

Coldhearted looked at Elizabeth. "I know, Mama. I know. But it's dangerous and I can't have none of y'all gettin' caught in the crossfire."

"You gonna spend up your trust," Elizabeth said to him. "You talkin' about buying up."

He smiled. "You worry too much."

He never spoke about his trust money nor did he let on to anyone about all of the cash he was stacking up from VULKANICKACYD, Savage Hoodz Records, Garters and his drug distribution network with the Crips on the streets.

There was a knock on the front door. Double Deuce and his cousins drew weapons. Coldhearted did the same thing before looking at the security monitors in the foyer.

"It's SHZ," Coldhearted told his boys.

He opened up the doors and in came Chubb, Dojo, Shadow Warrior, Choir Boy, Wolfman, Orca, Tommy Gun,

HK, Mac-11, Sonja, Alejandra, Shay, Joyce, Blue Eyez, Diamond Girl, Bhad Barbie, Sunny, Ava Applez and her girl-friend Juicy-P.

"What's up, boy!" the 17 year old Barbie said in her cute little chipmunk voice.

Coldhearted greeted everyone. They all went and sat on the back deck since it was a nice and warm morning. Before she went out there, Barbie handed Coldhearted a fancy looking flash drive.

"What's the count on it?" he asked her quietly.

"It's a bunch of Bitcoin transfers from VULKAN purchases," the five foot even brown skin girl answered. "Your cut. After Rock passed we had to hack through all of his accounts and get to the cryptocurrency data. We were lucky to find the Bitcoin. Your slice is probably $117,200. All the data on what we all got is on there, too."

"I'll be right back," he said and went back to his bedroom. "Liza!" he called out.

She came back holding Isabel in her arms.

He looked at her. "Mami, remember I said my fuckin' Bitcoin was lost with Rock's demise?"

She nodded. "Yeah, so what happened?"

"They hacked his accounts," Coldhearted said as he plugged the drive into his laptop. He pulled up the records and saw the Bitcoin files. He immediately contacted his own banker in the Cayman Islands that instructed him to trade the

Bitcoin for cash ASAP and deposit it into his account. "It's worth about $117K, he told Liza."

"Dang, that's good!" She exclaimed.

He kissed her cheek. "Mama... call my lawyer for me and tell her we need help to move. To buy up."

"Boy you keep telling me to do it," Liza said as she took the laptop. "You do it with me. How much to sell for?"

"Just call Melissa Verducci," he said. "She'll help get it rolling wit' the real estate agent."

He went back out to the SHZ men and women. He embraced Chubb. "How you doing, son?"

Chubb exhaled and shrugged. "I'm here..."

Barbie spoke for the group. "We was wonderin' what was gonna happen to VULKANIKACYD, the record company, and everything else since..."

"And leadership," Diamond Girl added. "Chubb already told us he wants no responsibility like that."

Coldhearted and Tommy looked at Chubb.

"I said it, Chubb conveyed to them. "Rock has all these cars, leases and record contracts and shit I ain't tryna pay or even understand."

"Don't worry about it," Coldhearted assured him. "Me and Tommy are the new bosses. And since ya moms is silent partner Rock will still get a duffel bag full of cash every month.

"The feds is onto VULKANIK," Tommy told everybody. "So, we goin' black. Any cellphone, computer, tablet or device ever connected to it bring it to headquarters today. And waste no time. Move all y'all shit outta HQ by 7 o'clock PM tomorrow and get far away from it."

"Why?" Juicy-P asked. "That place is like home!"

"It'll be an inferno," Coldhearted informed them.

Shadow hung his head. "What about VULKANIK? That shit had us splitting over a million a month."

"We'll rebuild it elsewhere – by another name," Tommy guaranteed them. "It's just so dangerous right now. Lay low, don't use any emails connected to VULKANIK or nothin'. The FBI will lock ya ass up. Meanwhile, everyone bring those devices to HQ. Move ya shit out."

"What about the hangout loft?" Diamond Girl queried.

Coldhearted answered that. "That's still ours."

Dojo slapped hands with HK and Coldhearted before saying, "Damn I was worried my nygga!"

Coldhearted waited for the fat brown skinned 19 year old computer genius to explain.

"I been sleeping at HQ cuz I'm homeless," Dojo admitted. "I spend so much time writing code, bussin' down firewalls, directing VULKANIK merch... it made no sense to keep my crib."

Coldhearted nodded. "I know alotta y'all stay there... Sunny's moms put her out, Choir Boy pops threw him out, Joyce, Blue Eyez – so what? We family. No one is puttin' any of y'all out. We about to do something even bigger. Just handle what Tommy said to handle. Then stay at the hangout or whatever."

"Please tell me none of y'all are broke," Tommy said, looking around the group.

"We ain't broke," Barbie said. "Rock was the only one buying hundred thousand dollar cars. No offense, Chubb."

Chubb shook his head. "Don't worry 'bout it."

"Everyone meet at SHZ Records Friday morning at 9 AM," Tommy said.

"Friday morning?" Diamond girl, the thick and beautiful white girl mimicked.

"There's a big conference room there," Tommy told them. "We gon' turn it into a computer room."

They ended the meeting there.

As they were leaving they were being observed by detectives who were taking down their license plate numbers and snapping pictures of everyone's face in the group.

Unbeknownst to the detectives OG Bobby Tate had spotted them when he arrived in his tricked out 1961 Riviera. Its coat was a beautiful metallic obsidian black, the chrome Toyo tires along with the custom chrome monster grill up front made it worthy of an appearance in one of the fast and furious movies.

Tate was in the car with the three of his closest goons from South Central. They were also Rollin 60s Crips but these cats were bonafide assassins. Ammo, Kaz, and Cumba.

Not many West Coast dudes wore dreads but these three all wore dreads that came down to their shoulders.

"C," Tate said when he called him.

"Yep."

"Police outside takin' pics of anyone comin' or goin' from ya crib," Tate informed him.

"Aight," C replied. "Lay low at HQ for now."

Chapter Forty-Four

Liza & Coldhearted's House
The Feds Visit

"Change of plans," Coldhearted said to Elizabeth and Liza. "Y'all got ya passports and everything in order, right?"

Liza sucked her teeth. "We all got our passports together, Papi. Why?"

"Call Lupé," Coldhearted said as he walked into their closet and returned with a bank bag. He emptied the contents of the bag onto the bed. There was a stack of rubber banded debit and credit cards along with $10,000 in cash. Take Lupé with y'all on vacation."

Elizabeth slowly sat down on the soft black leather sofa near the large windows in their master bedroom. She wanted to pry but all that would do is anger Sage. So, she just sent a text to Lupé asking if she wanted to go on vacation with her, Liza, the baby, and Lilly.

"Vacation where?" Liza inquired, the idea appealing to her. "And you mean me, Liz, Izzy, and Lilly. Not you?"

"I promise to follow in a week," he assured her. "You are Dominicana and Boriqua. Why don't y'all choose either country and while there find us a little beach house to vacation at? Get a bangin' place to stay, pamper yourselves at the finest spas get them pretty feet done cuz they look like monkey toes right now."

"They do not! Liza laughed and looked down at her small bare feet. "I can be a *foot* model!"

"I know, I know." He said. And to prove it he got down on his knees, bent down to the floor and kissed her feet. "See?"

Elizabeth was amused. "This is gettin' weird. Y'all need me to leave the room?"

Lisa hugged her man. "I love you, Papi. One week, right?"

"One week. *Una semana.*"

Liza opened up her laptop. "Auntie, let's go to the Dominican Republic. And since Puerto Rico is not far we can fly there from San Pedro de Macoris. Look at all of the beautiful beaches and coastal resorts and mansions on top of the cliffs there."

Coldhearted left them there and put a call through to

nearby "Donut N Coffee" coffee stop. He asked them to deliver a deluxe box of 24 assorted donuts and several large coffees - sugar and creamer on the side - as soon as possible. Fifteen minutes later a blonde teenage girl arrived in a Honda Civic. Coldhearted pointed her to the cops sitting in the unmarked Hyundai up the street.

"The gray one?" she asked.

Coldhearted nodded. "Yeah and tell them if they ever need anything else in this world... come to me. Tell 'em just like that."

She nodded.

"Whattaya gonna tell 'em?" he asked.

The young girl repeated it to him. "He says: if you need anything else in this world to come to me." Tell 'em just like that.

He gave the girl a $100 bill. "Keep the change."

"Oh, my goodness! Thank you!" she gushed.

She then reached into her car and pulled out the box containing the donuts and she placed the carton which held four large hot coffees on top of it she walked up the street and the window came down on the passenger side. Coldhearted watched the police take the coffee and donuts and try to tip the high schooler. She declined and walked back to her car. The cops waved at Coldhearted and he sent them a soldier's salute.

"It's official," Coldhearted to Deuce, Double J and

Spooky. The cops and feds are watchin'. So, no crime right now."

Coldhearted had secret compartments installed inside of his house where his weapons were hidden and he kept no narcotics there so he could certainly survive a police search. He collected all burner phones and devices as Tommy had instructed and directed Deuce to destroy them in a steel barrel fire in the backyard.

Lupé arrived later in the day. She took Liza, Elizabeth and Lilly to the salon and the mall. It was right after that when Coldhearted received a visit from three members of the local and federal taskforce assembled subsequent to the southside bombing.

"Officers," Coldhearted said looking each of the three men in the eyes.

"I'm Sergeant John Holland of the Mt. Vernon Police Department," the cop introduced himself as he observed the young man standing in front of him and the attractive 40-plus white woman who stood behind him. "Sage Thomas?"

Coldhearted nodded yes. "Come on in."

They were all lead into the living room where all of them took seats. Coldhearted sat next to his attorney who just so happenedd to come by to help him with a list of matters concerning moving, finances, and other legal issues.

"This is Melissa Verducci, my family attorney." He introduced her. "Funny how it worked out, huh?"

Sergeant Holland agreed. "It actually speeds things up

for our investigation because you're a minor and for us to speak to you... it's best to have an attorney or guardian present."

"And you two," Coldhearted said to the other two clean cut white men sitting with their legs crossed and hands in their laps.

"Special Agent Jim Mulligan and Special Agent Carter Hayes," Holland introduced them.

"Okay," Coldhearted said. "What's up? Why are you here?"

"The Southside car bombings," Holland told him.

"I had nothin' to do with it," Coldhearted denied it.

Holland held up a hand. "Hold on, son. We know all about what happened with Rock and the ongoing feud between the Bloods gang and Savage Hoodz gang."

"Savage Hoodz is a record label not a gang," Coldhearted said pointing at a big portrait that hung over the fireplace.

The MVPD Sergeant looked over at it. Clearly that's what the Savage Hoodz logo was. It was set inside of a record with a faceless hooded man inside of it who was pointing a M16 machine gun at the person looking at the portrait.

"I see," Holland said turning back around. "Who is *D-Slice?*"

Coldhearted shrugged one moment but then he said, "I heard the name. Not sure where."

"The Bloods say he was murdered," Holland revealed. "I'm laying it out for you, son. The killing of D-Slice prompted the retaliation against Rock. And we think the Savage Hoodz, who are now heavily aligned and allied with the Crips, bombed those cars on the Southside."

"Okay this is gone on long enough," Melissa said holding her hand up. "He denied being part of that."

"Hold up, Ms. V," Coldhearted intervened. He handed the sergeant his phone after bringing up security camera footage files of him and the funeral party guests at Garters. "All my peoples were present... and I'm sure you'll do a deep dive into each of us. None of us has bombmaking knowledge. Give me an e-mail I'll send you a full week's worth of our files there."

"Twenty-four hours worth will do it," the Sergeant said.

"No, we'll take the week's worth, sir," Agent Hayes requested peering over at Holland.

Coldhearted didn't care. SHZ had some of the best young hackers on the East Coast down with them. They had managed to doctor the time and date stamps so it appeared as though Tate, Tommy, and Shadow had never left the funeral party during the bombings. So, when the feds analyzed the video they would now see that the entire SHZ and known Crips in Mt. Vernon all had ironclad alibis.

"We have a bomb-sniffing K9 unit outside," Sergeant Holland said. "You wouldn't mind if we walked him through your car's garage and-"

"No, no, no," Melissa stated adamantly. "That is a search and that will not happen without a warrant. Absolutely no search will occur without a warrant. He gave you his alibi. We're done here."

Coldhearted said no more.

Melissa ushered the men out of the house and that was the end of that.

Chapter Forty-Five

The Farnum Rd Stashhouse
Mt. Vernon, NY
Thursday 6 PM

With Liza, Elizabeth, Lupé, Isabel and Lilly vacationing in the Dominican Republic, Coldhearted hired moving crews to haul everything off to storage inside of their Mt. Vernon house. Once that was completed, another crew came in to start the renovations and cleanup.

Coldhearted decided that it would actually be best if he kept the house since it was already fully paid for. It made better sense to upgrade it, have it appraised and refinanced.

He was certain that he could receive at least $600,000 to $750,000 for it because of the current housing market prices and the previous additions made to it when it was rebuilt after the fire.

On the fifth day of the renovations a second company arrived at the house and put up the nine-foot, blue colored, wrought iron gates which surrounded the property. In between each ten foot section of the gate they erected black brick beams to strengthen the gate. Out front an electronic pair of gates that opened inwards were installed. A security company came next to put in a state-of-the-art security system outside of the house as well as inside. This included turning one of the bathrooms into a panic room.

Coldhearted had to break his promise to Liza to meet her and the others in the Dominican Republic. When he explained everything to her she was actually excited.

"A laser beam security system?" she asked him during a Skype call.

"And a panic room," he said.

"At least we ain't movin'. I like our house."

"Me, too," he agreed. "You ain't gon' recognize it."

"You paint it?"

"Yep."

"Sage!" she cried. "For real? Show me. Take the laptop outside and lemme see!"

"Nope. I'll see you when you get back or when I get there."

He went to Savage Hoodsz Records over on Richlee Boulevard where he had a safe stashed securely in one of the downstairs offices there. It was filled with rubber-banded $500 stacks of drug loot from all of the ecstasy, meth, cocaine, heroin and K2 sales. It wasn't a whole lot there. $24,500. He called up Tate.

"What up with it, nygga?" Tate answered.

"Meet me over F-R wit everybody," Coldhearted said. "I ain't got no tail. Make sure-"

"Nygga you already!" Tate growled and ended the call.

Ten minutes later Coldhearted had parked the gray Pontiac he had rented in an alley a block away from Farnum Road which is what "F-R" meant. He traipsed on through the alley and used a key to let himself into the backyard of his stash house. The two white pitbulls he kept there had smelled him coming before he had even arrived. They were absolutely going nuts from excitement.

Not wanting to make them even more excited he made no eye contact with them until he re-locked the gate. Then he made them sit down on the back porch. He bent down between them and patted them down while they licked his face.

"Stop," He ordered them. "Where yo tongue been, girl? In her ass? I don't know where y'all tongue been!" He laughed.

They just barked and whined. Happy to see him.

"Y'all wanna move today?" He asked them as he pulled out two leashes.

They saw the leashes and wagged their tails. He put the leashes on them and let them into the back door of the stash house.

Tate, Deuce, Double J, Spooky, and the three assassins Tate brought in from South Central – Ammo, Kaz and Cumba - arrived shortly after Coldhearted. By that time Coldhearted had already emptied out the contents of the safe and secured closet. He was sitting inside of the living room with several duffel bags on the floor.

Tate must have been in the middle of getting his hair braided because it was only halfway done. The 5 feet 7 inch smoky black Bobby Tate only had on a white wife beater so his big muscles bulged out menacingly.

"Kaz, Ammo, Cumba," Coldhearted acknowledged them with a nod. He looked at the three black assassins with the dreads. "Y'all good out here?"

"It ain't L.A.," Kaz stated with his West Coast accent. "The hotties is bad though.

"Well, look," Coldhearted said as they each took seats around the living room. He looked at Tate. "New Rochelle is two towns away. Y'all ever heard of the Regency Park Apartments out there?"

They all looked at each other and shook their heads no.

"It's low income housing for women with kids," Coldhearted told them. "All our people let's focus them over there.

Most of these cats is comin' over with their chicks and kids so it's shit like that we have to overtake. It's brand new apartments. Two, three and four bedrooms."

They all thought it was a good idea.

"We know people we can bribe to get all the applications approved," Coldhearted assured them. "Word life. That's number one. Number two is White Oak Mobile Homes. Brand new rentals. It's like eighty of those about a mile from my house. Same thing. They both about to take applications and we can flood them. But it gotta be now."

"How much rent we talkin'?" Kaz asked.

"Son," Coldhearted shrugged. "For women with kids they'll have to pay a couple hundred a month."

Ammo nodded, twirling one of his shoulder length dreads. "Yeah, we gotta get the gang settled in tight, cuz. It's a gold mine out here if we can get the heat off of us."

"Time gonna do that, cuz," Tate told them.

Coldhearted nodded. "My lawyer's sister works in the H.U.D. office here in Westchester so we payin' her off to give favoritism to our applicators."

"You mean *applicants*," Tate corrected.

"All y'all except Deuce, Jay and Spook got kids," Coldhearted added on." Get y'all's chicks at attention. The Crips set up shop in spots like that, no need to worry 'bout ya nosey neighbor being a nosey neighbor. Word. Cuz he ya homie."

"Okay," Tate said. "What's wit da bags?"

"That Riviera you rollin' in is something serious," Coldhearted said. "Until the heat die down use rentals. Y'all shit too flashy and we need to be low."

Tate was given a credit card bearing the same SHZ Inc./Bobby Tate. "Against the company's account?" Tate asked.

Coldhearted nodded. "And I need something from you nyggaz."

Tate looked at him. "Us? Whattaya mean us?"

Kaz, Ammo, Cumba, Deuce, Spooky and Double J each looked at one another and then back at the big 16 year old Coldhearted.

"Yeah," he said to them. I wanna be a Rollin 60 Neighborhood Crip."

OG Bobby Tate chuckled along with Kaz, Cumba and the others.

That angered Coldhearted. "What da fuck's funny?"

"Nuttin. Just tell us somethin' we don't know, homie," Tate said, standing up. "We gotchu, nygga. But we takin' a trip out West to do it."

"I don't give a fuck where it's at," Coldhearted slyly smiled. As long as it gets done."

Tate stared at him. "We know you a gangster already but you still need to put in some fresh work."

"Yeah. I got just the thing in mind," Coldhearted stated with a sinister look in his eyes. "It's time to clean up the loose ends..."

Chapter Forty-Six

"**W**here's y'all's regular cellphones at, son?" Coldhearted asked Tommy and Shadow Warrior.

They were inside of the manager's office at Garters the next day. Tommy and Shadow produced their expensive cell phones Coldhearted pulled out his own. He dropped all three phones into a lock box, secured the box and placed it into the safe.

"Whatta we doin'" Tommy quickly asked. "I hate bein'

without my phone."

"Remember that cartel plug Rock have hooked up for us?" Coldhearted asked them.

Shadow and Tommy nodded.

"Look," Coldhearted pull out a burner phone and showed them a text message he'd received.

The message on the screen said: *Mr. B will continue to do everything in memory of Rob but a face to face first in S.D. No devices. Bring other partners will have to meet later. R owed 500K after last meet.*

"Aight... where's 'S.D.?'" Shadow inquired.

"San Diego," Coldhearted replied. "California."

"Dat nygga owed five hunnit bandz?" Tommy asked.

"You sound surprised," Coldhearted retorted.

Tommy shook his head exasperatedly. "It's a lot in my cash is tied up."

Coldhearted glared at Tommy. "What da fuck you doin' wit all ya cash, homie?"

Tommy thought it over. "I'm gonna need a week or two. We need to pay them the five double oh *and* come up with what to set us straight for the street?"

"It's all consignment," Coldhearted admitted. "They know we Garters owners. We basically goin' out there to put the club up as collateral."

Tommy rubbed his hands together. "We gotta bring that shit back over?"

"We pick it up in Chicago," Coldhearted said. "We

gotta go."

Tommy and Shadow agreed and they all left the club. But when they reached his black rented Chevy Suburban out back in the parking lot Coldhearted cursed to himself.

"Shit!" he said checking his pockets. "I'll be right back."

He ran back to the office and, clandestinely, retrieved Tommy and Shadows cellphones. He placed them into a black plastic bag after turning them on. He made his way out to the parking lot and hopped into the Suburban.

"So, we flyin', or what?" Shadow asked as Coldhearted drove off.

"We gotta roll," he said. "As for them cats five hundred bandz I'll cover it this time, Tommy. But as a partner, you have to cover your end."

"You payin' cash to 'em?" Shadow inquired after a few seconds.

Coldhearted stopped at a red light and shook his head. "Overseas transfer," was all he said.

Ten minutes later they were in front of a house Tate had texted him the address too earlier that day. Tate, Deuce, Kaz, Cumba and Ammo all piled up inside of the Suburban and took off shortly after that.

Chapter Forty-Seven

Los Angeles, CA

5:30 PM

Before they had even gotten out of New York Coldhearted had stopped to fill the gas tank up at a Manhattan Shell gas station. While there a man wishing to make some extra change started cleaning the front windshield. Everyone else had went inside to make various purchases from the small grocery store there.

"Hey, man, c'mere," Coldhearted called the old timer over.

"Yes, sir," the man answered as the big teenage boy

handed him a ten dollar bill and the black bag with the two cell phones in it.

"Go pawn 'em off to drug dealers," Coldhearted directed him. "The service is on and they's unlocked. No questions. *Just walk!*"

The old hustler didn't just walk he nearly ran.

It's gonna be hot out that bitch in? Tommy who was riding shotgun ask as he looked at his watch. It was almost 7 PM.

"Hell yeah," Tate said.

"Stop along the way so we can shop, nygga," Shadow called up front from the rear passenger's seat.

"Go down New Jersey Turnpike," Tate instructed Coldhearted once they hit the city. When the GPS shows you Pennsylvania Turnpike, on Exit 6, hop on I-76 and just drive West."

Coldhearted turned the music up and said, "Aight, let's get it."

The trip would take four days.

THE ROAD TRIP had taken four days with all the hotel stops they made. But eventually they rolled into Los Angeles smack dab during the middle of rush hour traffic.

Coldhearted, now seated in the front passenger seat, was listening to Tate as he explained a lot about the congested, bustling, "City of Angels." Tommy and Shadow listened in from the rear of the luxury Suburban.

"We about to enter South-Central now, cuz," Tate said as he drove off the freeway.

"Why they call it South-Central?" Coldhearted wanted to know.

"Man, I lived out here and I don't know dat shit!" Deuce revealed.

"That's because you whatn't driving," Tate reasoned. What a lotta L.A. cats don't know is when the term South Central is used it refers specifically to the area of Slauson, extending South through the Compton city and Compton's areas. The East-West borders are basically the Harbor Freeway on the West and the Long Beach Freeway to the East that's really it."

Kaz added on his two cents. "And South-Central is made-up of Compton, East Compton, Florence, Athens, Willow-brook and Carson."

Tate drove through Slauson Avenue and turned up an alley to see if they were being followed. Within minutes they were pulling up on Gage Street and Central Avenue.

"Y'all stretch ya legs," Tate said to everyone. "Deuce come say what up to ya auntie."

While Tate and Duece ran inside of the old, ugly, lime green-colored house a huge Doberman Pincher ran up to the fence near where they were parked and started barking at them. Coldhearted looked inside of the McDonald's bag they'd saved from earlier and removed two uneaten Big Macs. He walked close enough to the fence and tossed one of the sandwiches over it.

The large beast gobbled the entire thing down in a matter of seconds.

"You gon' and shut the fuck up?" Coldhearted teased the animal. "Sit!" He commanded the big dog.

"The mufucka only sittin' cuz he hungry," Cumba stated.

Coldhearted waited a minute. "Good boy!"

He threw the second Big Mac over the fence.

Now, the dog just stared at the men who were leaning against the black Chevy Suburban. Moments later he just laid down and kept his eyes open.

"Aight y'all," Tate said as he stepped out of the house with a huge bowl of fried chicken.

The Doberman snarled and started barking again.

Tate passed the home fried chicken out to everyone and gave the ball back to his sister who came outside to be nosey. She waved hi to the men and they thanked her for the delicious food.

Deuce came out and hugged his aunt Marietta. "We in town so we'll be back," Deuce told her.

Tate took the wheel again and pulled away before Marietta started asking too many questions.

"So, what's the play?" Tommy inquired, yawning. "I mean... when we goin' to San Diego to meet the Mexicans?

"You in a rush big dog?" Coldhearted smiled back.

"We've been gone four days already," Tommy stated with a shrug.

"We doin' a multi million dollar drug deal and dis nygga complainin'," Coldhearted turned to Tate and said, his voice filled with sarcasm.

Tommy sucked his teeth. "Nygga I'm just saying because you said don't call back home, we left our phones - I got a kid and a girl, and family waiting on me. Ain't nobody fuckin' complainin' mufucka!"

Coldhearted turned in his seat. "Who da *fuck* you talkin' to like that?!"

"You, nygga! You talkin' to me like I'm ya fuckin' puppet or something!" Tommy Gunz snapped. "You better go 'head wit that."

"Aight, we here," Tate interjected. "Y'all keep that fire up, cuz."

The vehicle stopped on 92nd Street and Central Avenue, not far from his sister's house on Gage Street.

"Why, what's this?" Tommy looked at the yellow house they were parked in front of.

"Party time," Kaz remarked as he got out of the truck.

They locked the truck up and walked along the side of the house to the back gate. There was a gate they had to go through which put them out onto a walkway that guided them across a narrow alley and into a building marked "Bingo Hall."

As they entered, it was clear that this was no bingo hall.

There were about three dozen men and women inside yelling at the two women who were going at each other's heads in bare knuckle combat!

Tate looked at Tommy Gunz. Welcome to Fight Club!" Tate yelled over all the noise.

"This is cool and all but I ain't come to fight," Tommy declined.

"Too late for that!" Kaz coldly stated. "No one leaves without bleeding in this club. Once you walk in you're *locked* in."

Tommy looked at Shadow Warrior.

They looked at Coldhearted.

"What?" Coldhearted said. "I didn't make the rules."

Coldhearted took off his shirt...

Chapter Forty-Eight

The "Bingo Hall"
Los Angeles, CA
6:20 PM

The bulldykes beat one another so bad that they ended up knocking each other out! Their lips and eyes were a bloody mess. The way the rules apparently went was when one fight was over the "Promoter" would come out and simply seek the next man or woman who wanted to battle...

"Who's next?!" The promoter would walk around and sneer. "Do you want to be the *challenger* or the *challenged?!*"

If someone was challenged by the challenger it was *mandatory* that they fight or they would be jumped. And, in the past, some of those who had gotten jumped bones, brain damage, and even death. Tommy and Shadow couldn't believe that they'd been suckered into this crazy shit.

Finally, the Promoter caught Coldhearted's eye and Coldhearted waved him over.

"You up?" The Promoter asked. He was a bald-headed brown skinned Crip. He had the Rolling 60s tattoos on full display as he wore a black wife beater.

"One thousand on me," Coldhearted stated as he waved the clip of $100 bills around.

"How old you is?"

"Sixteen."

The Promoter shook his head. "You a big ass youngsta. But you have killa all in ya eyes..."

When the last fight was over the Promoter placed $1000 in bets for Coldhearted. Then he was made to choose who he was going to fight.

Coldhearted walked straight up to Tommy and pointed at him. Tommy shook his head, feeling like Coldhearted had crossed the line and flipped on some other shit. Tommy felt betrayed by his friend.

Tommy took his shirt off and got a squeal of approval from the few women who were there that weren't dykes.

"READY?!" the Promoter yelled. "FIGHT!"

Coldhearted was a big boy but he was a Floyd

Mayweather Jr.-style fighter, with a bit of that 1988 Mike Tyson grit in him. Tommy threw a flurry of punches at cold hearted and connected to the chest and face with two of them.

"C'mon, nygga," Coldhearted taunted him.

Tommy was a beast with his hands but Coldhearted also knew that he drank a lot, smoke too many blunts and cigarettes. A nygga like that could only go for so long before his chest burned or he caught stomach cramps.

Tommy kept swinging but he was also missing. Coldhearted stood back and counterpunched. After several minutes Tommy was sweating and breathing hard. Coldhearted advanced and caught him with his mouth open. *CRAAACCKK!* Tommy stumbled backward and Coldhearted *jump-kicked* him between his wide open legs! Tommy was not expecting a dirty low blow like that and it all but ended everything!

Tommy fell to his knees and wanted to crumble up like a piece of paper, but he got stuck in the kneeling position. Coldhearted rushed up to him and sledge hammered his right fist across the left side of Tommy's face!

SMAASSHH! Tommy fell over and the ground met the right side of his face. He looked at tape, mouthing the words, *"Let's do it."*

"The winner!" The promoter yelled, collecting all the bets.

Coldhearted was handed the $2000 but he yelled, *"Bet*

two thousand!"

Then he waved in Shadow Warrior.

"We gotta do this, bro?" Shadow asked him.

"This is what I don't like about you nyggas!" Coldhearted snapped at Shadow. "You cryin' and complaining ass SHZ nyggaz. Always whinin' at the site or prospect of blood, pain and violence! Miss me with that soft shit and let's get it poppin' nygga! Word to mutha."

As they started fighting Tommy was dragged off the floor with the severely cracked neck. Coldhearted brought that Mike Tyson out of retirement. He saw the fear in Shadow Warrior's eyes and fed off of it.

He crouched down and bum rushed Shadow! Raining bonecrunching face blow after face blow on him! A left to the right eye, cracking the eye socket! A right cross over the bridge of the nose, fracturing it and causing it to bleed! But Shadow could take a beating! His lip busted open at the top and then at the bottom before a Shadow spit out two teeth that got knocked out.

"Coldhearted! Tate yelled, breaking his concentration and devastation.

Coldhearted looked over at Tate and saw that there were only a small group of people there now: Tate, Deuce, Kaz, Cumba, Ammo, Coldhearted, the Promoter AKA "Bump", Icepick, Nitro, Forty 7, Ceeze and Flush. All of them were about Tate's age and we're Rollin 60s Neighborhood Crips.

"These nyggas is hurt," Tate said, indicating Tommy who was laid out on the floor moaning and groaning. "It's time."

Tate had Tommy brought over to the center of the fight floor and placed over industrial plastic sheeting. Then he was gagged and tied up with his hands behind his back. Next, they did the same thing to Shadow who struggled more to get free.

Coldhearted had known all the while that he would assassinate Tommy eventually. There was no fucking way in hell he was going to share Garter/SHZ, Inc. with him and there was definitely zero way that Coldhearted would could ever sleep at night - or at any time for that matter - knowing that Tommy and Shadow had had a hand in those bombings.

OG Bobby Tate was a different kind of monster entirely. Plus, he was Coldhearted's Capo. Deuce his Lieutenant. The Blue Wave takeover was well underway on the East Coast. At least in Mount Vernon it was.

These nyggas is loose ends, Coldhearted thought as he removed his gleaming machete from the scabbard attached to his back. Even the seasoned gangsters in the private room were squeamish when they saw that sharp chrome colored blade get pulled out. A few of the men had to keep their bubble guts in check as well. Nerves were getting to them.

Coldhearted wasted no time.

Tate, Kaz and Cumba held Tommy tightly down on his stomach as Coldhearted stood off to one side and raised the blade named "Miss Heartless." He did three practice chops before bringing her down hard like the hammer of Thor!

"Ohhh shittt!!!!" Three or four men yelled in unison.

Tommy's head rolled over to the side and stared off into Infinity with a blank stare.

Next was Shadow Warrior. It took a second shot to take his head but the deed was done! Coldhearted used his handkerchief to wipe the blade clean while the bodies we're being tightly wrapped up. Once that was completed, the bodies were dragged out.

"You see what it is, right?" Tate said to Coldhearted. And then he looked around to all those within his tight knit Rolling 60s Neighborhood Crip family. This young nygga a fucking boss back East! He a born Bloodhunter... And y'all see what he can do with his hands. And his favorite weapon is a machete. Now he want to be Rollin 60."

Deuce, his main man, came out of nowhere and started the vicious pummeling! Then Tate, followed by Kaz, and Cumba, then Ammo! Soon Coldhearted was caught inside of a human gauntlet of powerful flying fists!

Bump, Icepick, Nitro, Forty-7, Ceeze and Flush thrashed him and pounded him into the ground! Not feeling sorry for him nor having any mercy at all, they all stood him up and beat him until his eyes were swollen shut and his face was bloody and leaking.

Inches away from dying he thought about Liza, Isabel and Lilly...

Then it all went dark.

To be continued...

COLDHEARTED 2

Coming Soon

Did you enjoy the read?
Let us know how much by leaving us a review on Amazon
and Goodreads.

Keep reading for a preview of...

Hittaz: Get It Back In Blood
By Lou Garden Price, Sr.

Chapter One

The Villa Strip club*East New York*BKNY*Monday
12:00 A.M.

Joker Red was what everyone called him, but his government name was David Leon Hodges. He was a light-skinned black man, thirty-one years of age, with green eyes and powerfully built. He had a single gold tooth and wavy hair; the women loved him at first glance. He sat quietly in the rear left backseat of the sleek new 2020 Buick Century as his first cousin and business partner Skeeter Dukes weaved in and out of the late evening traffic on Atlantic Avenue near Brooklyn's Fort Greene Section.

Skeeter passed a lit blunt of purple haze to their closest comrade, Ghostman Dinero, who sat shotgun.

"You good, Red?" Black N9NE, who was seated behind Ghostman, inquired. "How's it feel to be outta the joint?"

Joker acknowledged him with a slow nod. "Exhilarating."

The four men had been close since pissy pampers in childhood and all of them were a part of a crew called "EVERYTHING IS EVERYTHING" or EIE—a Brooklyn gang they'd started back when they were still in middle school. Now they were all in their 20s and 30s, with Joker being the eldest at thirty-one, and the only one of the four who had been to prison.

EIE had been through hell together. They had fought in the military together - - where they'd lost comrades together, yet one amongst them had betrayed Joker to the pigs. The entire time he spent on the inside, he'd breathed hatred and vowed vengeance against the Judas who'd sold him down the river for thirty pieces of silver.

They were members of a highly organized stick-up crew that robbed and killed drug bosses, and on most occasions, they hit banks. Because robbing and kidnapping drug king-pins was so profitable, EIE had set up their own lucrative drug dealing network in Brooklyn, to sell the stolen merch. Four years ago, however, Joker had been caught after he had just firebombed a jacked SUV that had been used in a bank hold-up earlier that day. He was able to burn all the bank robbery evidence, including the disguise he had worn, along with the gas-saturated car, so the armed robbery charges could not stand without physical evidence linking him to the crime scene—especially when the state's best witness had failed to identify any of the EIE members in a police lineup. Therefore, Joker had escaped his most serious charges and had to be given a plea bargain on the arson and grand theft auto charges, which was a slap in the face to prosecutors and the police. Subsequently, he was sentenced to o to 4 years in state prison.

Now, he was free. And to celebrate his release, his entire crew were headed to the Villa Strip club in East New York to get their party on.

Skeeter turned down the Rick Ross club banger and looked into the rearview mirror at Joker. "Since you were doing time up north, I expanded the crew."

Joker glanced behind them. "I see the five car fleet."

"Yeah."

"Nice cars," Joker commented. "You always liked the flash. I hate it. The prisons are filled with niggas who like flash. You know what they do now?"

Skeeter sighed sarcastically. "No, but you'll tell me."

"They are all broke. They call home on expensive phone calls to broke black families, begging for ten and twenty dollar money orders. The fuckin' flash gets the attention of the law, who never see you going to a job. They know, because you tell 'em, that you doin' crime when you roll down the street in a hundred thousand dollars in vehicles."

Skeeter didn't want to argue. "They're basic cars."

Joker stared behind them once again.

A Ford Expedition.

A Buick LeSabre.

A Honda Accord.

A Nissan Pathfinder.

And the Buick Century.

Each of them were last year's editions. All black.

In Joker's view, the fleet was anything but basic.

"Most of them we know from Fort Greene ," Skeeter explained as they stopped at a red light on Rockaway Avenue and Livonia Avenue in Brownsville. "Others we know from school and the military. All are hittaz, killaz, stickup men and plain ole miscreants. Wolves thrown back like fish in the sea by Uncle Sam, with nothing but horrifying memories of war and atrocities from over there. You remember Baghdad, Kandahar, Lybia, battles with Al Qaeda, ISIL and others?"

"Can't forget it," Joker recalled. "Especially the *others*."

The warriors in the car were quiet, somber, at Joker's words. They were all haunted by the same memories.

"I figure it like this," Ghostman said as they rolled down New Lots Avenue and into East New York, turning left onto Pennsylvania Avenue. "We were over there killin' people with skin the same color as ours, and they were poorer than we could ever be. So, I may as well come home and kill some no good black mufuckas who sell dope that ain't poor."

"Makes sense to me," Black N9NE added.

They turned another left onto Livonia and parked in front of the Villa. Skeeter climbed out of the car and stretched as he adjusted his Gucci glasses on his brown-skinned face. Every member of EIE eventually surrounded the Buick Century and dapped each other.

While the sinister crew scanned the faces of each person in the crowd, Joker's eyes were busy studying the faces of the twenty-two-man squadron, carefully and calculatedly. Skeeter had been correct; most of the men were familiar comrades. There was, of course, Joker's brother Big Al; Khadafi who was Skeeter's cousin and right hand; there was Fly, Jeff Lightfoot, Boo, Knarf, Blaze, Hard Knox, Bonecrusher, Broliks, Fast Eddie, Big Chief, Monk, Mustafa, Ground War, A-Son, Divine The God and one face Joker was not familiar with...

"Who is he?" Joker asked Skeeter.

"I'm Meth Man Ace," the tall man answered after overhearing Joker's inquiry. "I was stationed at the Tenth Mountain Division, New York. I live in Atlantic Terminal."

"So I guess crystal meth is your specialty," Joker stated conversationally.

Ace nodded. "I can make a few more chemicals than meth, sir."

"Joker Red," he reminded him. "Call them whites 'sir,' not me."

"It's a big crew," Joker observed in earshot of Skeeter.

"Yep," Skeeter nodded. "And I'm runnin' it just fine, cuz."

Joker smiled at him. "Chill, duke. No need to get your panties in a bunch. You da man now. You run it."

"Damned good to see you home, Red!" Fast Eddie greeted him, shoving a thick bankroll into Joker's hand. The two old war comrades embraced.

Joker looked down at the money, and his face lit up. "You still any good at safecrackin', E?"

"Hence the name," Eddie returned. "The boys and me took up a small collection for you. Anything else you need, lemme know, baby."

"That's right, comrade," Joker nodded, appreciating the love. "Let's go on in and see some bitches."

A City Girls hit was banging up in the club, causing all the strippers to go buck wild.

They partied like they were rich when they were really just getting by. The "licks" were not lining up like they needed them to and some EIE members were becoming desperate. They had kids to feed, let alone themselves. In any event, tonight was a special night because of Red's release, and Skeeter meant to enjoy it. The City Girls song was followed by Da Baby's best hit as the EIE crew entered the main floor area.

The club shook with a feel good vibration. The twenty-two-man team was led upstairs by a honey-skinned redheaded goddess dressed in revealing pink plastic boy shorts that were riding high up into her thick derriere. She motioned for them to follow her upstairs to VIP, where they were obviously expected.

"Dayyyuuummmmmmm!" Ghostman exclaimed as her thick down south butt cheeks bounced up the stairs. The men could actually see the moist, dark pussy lips underneath the pink plastic crotch covering. "WOW. That's all I gotta say...wow."

She only smiled at the effect her body had on them as they all craned their necks to stare at her magnificence.

"Fuck, baby doll," Skeeter said into her ear as she passed out VIP passes to all of them. "Please tell me you're stayin' up here?"

"I'll be in and out, big guy," she promised, noticing Joker Red—the silent one. "I'm Uzenna Jade, your VIP hostess."

Girls were all over the place. Quality seating aligned the walls and floor areas. The booths were either small or large, decorated with opaque golden curtains that could be pulled closed for privacy. Tables had been spread out around the stage area for smaller groups of club goers yet the crew chose the large party booths to sit in. It wasn't long before the club's top female dancers converged on EIE.

"Who's the guest of honor?" asked a white girl named Brittani Dane. She reminded Joker Red of one of those stacked white girls inside Kream Magazine.

"Why, hello," she whispered as she sat next to Joker.

Joker, aloof, nodded her way. "Hey, beautiful."

"Should we go to a private room?"

"Nah, baby, just dance and do ya thang," Joker instructed her as the buckets of Ace of Spades came out. "Drink with me. That's all you gotta do."

For the next hour, they all had fun with the dozens of nude and near nude strippers. Uzenna Jade never did come to dance, and Joker didn't think she would either. She was obviously the club's most beautiful girl, making her its number one. She was a unique and special standout, so Joker had to summon her over to a private booth and close the curtains.

"You're not from New York, huh?" he pointed out.

"No. Mississippi," she informed him.

"A dangerously beautiful southern import," he commented.

She appreciated the compliment. "Thank you," she said as he covered her with his black leather blazer jacket.

"This may sound corny," he started. "But are you already spoken for?"

She suddenly stood up. "I need to get back to work."

Joker also got to his feet. "Hold up, baby. Just lemme say... I think you're different from all the others. I know I am. I'm a different breed altogether."

She opened up the curtains to the booth and paused. "I'm a long and complicated story."

She left his blazer in the chair and scurried off, leaving

him even more intrigued about her. Joker, feeling the effects of the alcohol, went back out on the floor to see his crew heavily engrossed with the strippers in VIP. He caught a fleeting sight of Skeeter heading towards the bathroom.

Joker decided to follow him. When he walked in, Skeeter was down on his knees in the first stall, vomiting his guts out.

"Aw, shit," Skeeter puked out loudly. "Damn!"

"You aight, cuz?" Joker asked, concerned.

"It's just the gin, homie," Skeeter breathed, his face still hovering over the toilet as the nausea hit him again.

"Ayo, my man," Joker whispered in his ear. "I know what you did."

"Wha—?" Skeeter turned to look up at Joker, but it was too late. The straight razor appeared from nowhere, swiftly slicing a deep red canal across Skeeter's throat from ear to ear. Blood spurted and sprayed from the jugular vein.

Skeeter tried to scream as he clutched his throat but instead fell backward onto the toilet seat, wide-eyed with fear as he convulsed. He stared up at his cousin, shocked.

"Why?!"

"You filthy rat bastard," Joker hissed at him with a cold, vengeful smile. "You put the jakes on me when I went to firebomb the getaway car. You were the only one that knew the spot I'd picked out to burn it! You made a grave mistake, cuz. You sent detectives. No way detectives would just happen upon an arson. I spent four years waitin' to kill you."

Before Skeeter could reply, he lost consciousness and bled out.

Once Joker was sure Skeeter was dead, he hoisted his body so that he sat up on the toilet seat and locked the stall. Then he leaped over to the neighboring stall wall and cleaned his hands in the sink. He used brown paper towels to wipe the walls of the stalls clean of fingerprints and wiped the blood off the floor as best as he could. He flushed the straight razor and the paper towels down the toilet before slipping out of the bathroom to rejoin the party.

Welcome home, Joker Red.

Coming Soon

Other Books By

URBAN AINT DEAD

Tales 4rm Da Dale

By **Elijah R. Freeman**

The Hottest Summer Ever

By **Elijah R. Freeman**

Despite The Odds

By **Juhnell Morgan**

Good Girl Gone Rogue

By **Manny Black**

Hittaz 1, 2 & 3

By **Lou Garden Price, Sr.**

Charge It To The Game 1 & 2

By **Nai**

A Summer To Remember With My Hitta

By **Nai**

A Setup For Revenge

By **Ashley Williams**

Ridin' For You

By **Telia Teanna**

The State's Witness 1 & 2

By **Kyiris Ashley**

Stuck In The Trenches

By **Huff Tha Great**

<u>Coming Soon From:</u>

URBAN AINT DEAD

The Hottest Summer Ever 2
By **Elijah R. Freeman**

THE G-CODE
By **Elijah R. Freeman**

How To Publish A Book From Prison
By **Elijah R. Freeman**

Tales 4rm Da Dale 2
By **Elijah R. Freeman**

Hittaz 4
By **Lou Garden Price, Sr.**

COLDHEARTED 2
By **Lou Garden Price, Sr.**

Good Girl Gone Rogue 2
By **Manny Black**

Coming Soon From

Despite The Odds 2
By **Juhnell Morgan**

The State's Witness 3
By **Kyiris Ashley**

Ridin' For You, Too
By **Telia**

Stuck In The Trenches 2
By **Huff That Great**

A Setup For Revenge 2
By **Ashley Williams**

Charge It To The Game 3
By **Nai**

Books by
URBAN AINT DEAD's C.E.O

<u>Elijah R. Freeman</u>

Triggadale 1, 2 & 3

Tales 4rm Da Dale

The Hottest Summer Ever

Murda Was The Case 1 & 2

Follow

Elijah R. Freeman
On Social Media

FB: Elijah R. Freeman

IG: @the_future_of_urban_fiction

www.ingramcontent.com/pod-product-compliance
Lightning Source LLC
Chambersburg PA
CBHW071239300726
48975CB00002B/479